JUDITH

JUDITH

BY

BETTY NEELS

MILLS & BOON LIMITED

15–16 BROOK'S MEWS
LONDON W1A 1DR

First published 1982
Australian copyright 1982
Philippine copyright 1982
Large Print edition 1984

© Betty Neels 1982

ISBN 0 263 10465 6

Set in Monophoto Plantin 16 on 18 pt.
16-0384

Made and printed in Great Britain by
Richard Clay (The Chaucer Press) Ltd,
Bungay, Suffolk

CHAPTER ONE

HALF past two o'clock in the morning was really not the time at which to receive a proposal of marriage. Judith Golightly swallowed a yawn while her already tired brain, chock-a-block with the night's problems, struggled to formulate a suitable answer. She was going to say no, but how best to wrap it up into a little parcel of kind words? She hated hurting people's feelings, although she was quite sure that the young man sitting in the only chair in her small office had such a highly developed sense of importance that there was little fear of her doing that. Nigel Bloom was good-looking in a selfconscious way, good at his job even though he did tend to climb on other people's shoulders to reach the next rung up the ladder, and an entertaining companion. She had gone out with him on quite a number of occasions by now and she had to admit that, but he had no sense of humour and she had detected small meannesses beneath his apparent open-handedness; she suspected that he spent money where it was likely to bring him the best return or to impress his companions. Would he be mean with the housekeeping, she wondered, or grudge her pretty clothes?

He had singled her out for his attention very soon after he had joined the staff at Beck's Hospital as a surgical registrar, although she hadn't encouraged him; she was by no means desperate to get married even though she was twenty-seven; she had had her first proposal at the age of eighteen and many more besides since, but somehow none of them had been quite right. She had no idea what kind of man she wanted to marry, for she had seldom indulged in daydreaming, but of one thing she was sure—he would have to be tall; she was a big girl, splendidly built, and she had no wish to look down upon a husband, if and when she got one.

She leaned against the desk now, since there was nowhere for her to sit, and remarked with a little spurt of unusual rage, 'Why do you sit down and leave me standing, Nigel? Do you feel so very superior to a woman?'

He gave a tolerant laugh. 'You're tired,' he told her indulgently. 'I've been on the go all day, you know, and you didn't come on duty until eight o'clock last evening—and after all, you don't have the real hard work, do you? Two night Sisters under you and I don't know how many staff nurses and students to do the chores.'

Judith thought briefly of the hours which had passed, an entire round of the Surgical Wing—ninety beds, men, women and children—every patient visited, spoken to, listened to; the reports from each ward read and noted; at least five minutes with each nurse in charge of a ward, going over the instructions for the night, and all this interrupted several times: two admissions, one for theatre without delay, a death, anxious relatives to see and listen to over a cup of tea because that made them feel more relaxed and gave them the impression that time was of no account, a child in sudden convulsions; housemen summoned and accompanied to a variety of bedsides, phone calls from patients' families—it had been never-ending, and there were more than five hours to go.

Her rage died as quickly as it had come; she was too weary to have much feeling about anything, and meanwhile there was Nigel, looking sure of himself and her, waiting for his answer. He must be mad, she told herself silently, asking a girl to marry him in the middle of a busy night.

She looked across at him, a beautiful girl with golden hair, sapphire blue eyes and a gentle mouth. 'Thank you for asking me, Nigel, but I don't love you—and I'm quite sure I never shall.' She rushed on because he was prepared to argue about it: 'Look, I haven't the time . . . I know it's my meal time, but I wasn't going to stop for it anyway . . .'

He got up without haste. 'The trouble

with you is that you're not prepared to delegate your authority.'

'Who to?' She asked sharply. 'Sister Reed's in theatre, Sister Miles is on nights off, there's a staff nurse off sick and Men's Surgical is up to its eye-balls—you've just been there, but perhaps you didn't notice?'

Nigel lounged to the door. 'Mountains out of molehills,' he said loftily. 'I should have thought it would have sent you over the moon—my asking you to marry me.' He gave her one of his easy charming smiles. 'I'll ask you again when you're in a better temper.'

'I shall still say no.'

His smile deepened. 'You only think you will. See that that man who's just been admitted is ready for theatre by eight o'clock, will you? And keep the drip running at all costs. I'm for bed.'

Judith watched him go, but only for a moment; even though she was supposed to be free for an hour she had no time to do more than write up her books and begin on the report for the morning. She yawned again, then sat down behind the desk and picked up her pen.

A tap on the door made her give an almost inaudible sigh, but she said, 'Come in,' in her usual pleasant unhurried manner, already bracing herself for an urgent summons to one or other of the wards. Her bleep was off, a strict rule for her midnight break, but that had never stopped the nurses bringing urgent messages. It wasn't an urgent message; a tray of tea and a plate of sandwiches, borne by one of the night staff nurses on her way back from her own meal. Judith put down her pen and beamed tiredly at the girl. 'You're an angel, Staff—I wasn't going to stop . . .'

'We guessed you wouldn't, Sister. Sister Reed's just back with the patient, so you can eat in peace.'

'Bless you,' said Judith. 'Ask her to keep an eye on that new man's drip, will you? I'll be circulating in about twenty minutes.'

The second half of the night was as busy as the first had been. She went off duty at last, yawning her pretty head off, gobbling breakfast, and then, because it was good for her, going for a brisk walk through the dreary streets to the small park with its bright beds of flowers and far too cramped playing corner for the children. She had the Night Superintendent for a companion, a woman considerably older than herself and into whose shoes it was widely rumoured she would step in a few years' time. Judith preferred not to think about that, indeed, when she had the leisure to consider her future, she found herself wondering why she didn't accept the very next proposal of marriage and settle the matter once and for all.

Sister Dawes was speaking and Judith struggled to remember what she had said; something about measles. She turned a blank face to the lady, who laughed and said: 'You're half asleep, Judith. I was telling you there's a measles epidemic on the way—a nasty one, I gather. We must keep our eyes open. I know you're on Surgical, but even measles patients can develop an appendix or perforate an ulcer—for heaven's sake, if you see a rash on anyone, whisk them away. You've had measles, of course?'

'I've no idea,' declared Judith. 'I should think so—everyone has, and besides, I never catch things.'

She remembered that three nights later. Earlier in the evening a young boy had been admitted with a suspected appendicitis; he had been flushed, his eyes and nose were running and his voice hoarse. Judith eyed him narrowly and peered inside his reluctantly opened mouth. Koplik's spots were there all right; she thanked heaven that he had been admitted to a corner bed and that only she and the staff nurse on duty had been anywhere near him. They moved him to a side ward, made him comfortable, and Judith left the nurse with him while she telephoned—the houseman on duty first, Sister Dawes next and finally the Admission Room. The Casualty Officer was new and it was his first post and he might be forgiven for overlooking symptoms which showed no rash at the moment, but the staff nurse should have been more alert. Judith was brief, severe and just as pleasant in her manner as she always was. She gave instructions that everything that had come in contact with the boy should be disinfected and that the nurse should change her uniform. 'I'll send someone down,' she ended, 'but don't let her touch anything until you've dealt with it.'

It took a little organising to find nurses to take over while the surgical staff nurse went away to do the same thing, and then Judith herself went to change, making sure that everything went into a laundry bag with a warning note pinned to it. It took a small slice out of her night and left her, as usual, short of time.

During the next ten days there were three cases of measles—the nurse who had been on duty in the Admission Room, a ward maid and one of the porters. Another four days to go, thought Judith with relief, and they'd all be in the clear.

It was on the very last day of the incubation period that she began to feel ill; a cold, she decided, only to be expected, since although it was late spring, the weather wavered from cold and wet to fine and warm; no two days had been alike, enough to give anyone a cold. She took some aspirin and went to bed when she came off duty instead of taking her usual walk, but she didn't sleep much. Her head ached and so did her eyes and her throat felt sore; she got up and made tea and took more aspirin. She felt better after that, and presently dressed and went down to her meal, to be greeted with several candid opinions as to her poor looks from her friends. It was the Medical Wing Night Sister, a rather prissy type Judith didn't much like, who observed smugly: 'You've got the measles.'

She was right, of course—she was one of those infuriating young women who always are. Judith was examined by the Senior Medical Consultant, who happened to be in the hospital, told to go to bed and stay there, and warned of all the complications which might take over unless she did exactly as she was told.

As she was a sensible young woman, she

obeyed him to the letter, and was rewarded by an attack of severe conjunctivitis and, just as that was subsiding, broncho-pneumonia. It took a couple of weeks to get the better of these, but she was a strong girl and disinclined to lie about in bed feeling ill, and in a minimum of time she was on her feet once more, still beautiful but a little on the pale side and a good deal slimmer than she usually was. The tinted glasses she still wore lent her a mysterious air and what with her wan looks she presented a picture to wring any man's heart. At least, Nigel seemed to think so; he had kept away from her until she was free of infection, but once she was back in the Sisters' sitting room, waiting to see what lay in store for her, he came to see her, more tiresomely cocksure than ever, quite certain that the mere sight of him would be enough for her to agree to marry him. She still tired easily; ten minutes of his self-important prosing gave her a headache, and she said rather crossly: 'Look, Nigel, I'm not quite myself yet, but I haven't changed my mind. Do go away and find

someone else—there must be dozens of girls
longing to marry you.'

He took her seriously. 'Oh, yes, I know
that—I could have anyone of them whenever
I liked, but I've made up my mind to marry
you and I dislike being thwarted.'

'Well, I'm thwarting you,' she declared
with something of a snap, and then: 'Nigel,
why do you ask me at such unsuitable
times? The middle of a busy night—that
time I was taking a patient to theatre, and
now ...'

He had got to his feet huffily. 'I can see
you're determined to be irritable. I won't
bother you until you've recovered your
temper. I've got tickets for that new Burt
Reynolds film this evening—I shall take
Sister Giles.'

'Have fun,' said Judith, and meant it,
although how anyone could have fun with
Ruth Giles, a spiteful cat of a girl if ever
there was one, was beyond her.

She was given a month's leave the next
day. She telephoned her parents, threw a
few clothes rather haphazardly into a case,

took leave of her friends, got into her Fiat 600, a tight squeeze but all she could ever afford, and set off home through a June morning the brilliance of which made even the streets of London look lovely.

The country looked even lovelier. Judith was making for Lacock in Wiltshire, and once through London and its suburbs and safely on to the M4, she kept going briskly until she turned off at the Hungerford roundabout on to the Marlborough road; it wasn't very far now and the road, although busy, ran through delightful country, and at Calne she turned into a small country lane and so to Lacock.

The village was old and picturesque, a jumble of brick cottages, half-timbered houses and jutting gables. Judith went down the High Street, turned into a narrow road and stopped in front of a row of grey stone houses, roomily built and in apple pie order. The door of the centre house was flung open as she got out of the car, and her father crossed the narrow pavement, followed by an elderly basset hound who pranced ponderously around them both and then led the way back into the house. The hall was long and narrow with a staircase at one side and several doors. Judith's mother came out of the end one as they went in.

'Darling, here you are at last! We've been quite worried about you, although that nice doctor who was looking after you said we had no need to be.' She returned Judith's kiss warmly, a woman as tall as her daughter and still good-looking. 'You're wearing dark glasses—are your eyes bad?'

'They're fine, love—I wear them during the day if the sun's strong and it makes driving easier. It's lovely to be home.' Judith tucked a hand into each of her parents' arms and went into the sitting room with them. 'A whole month,' she said blissfully. 'It was worth having measles!'

After tea she unpacked in the room she had had all her life at the back of the house, overlooking the long walled garden which her father tended so lovingly and already filled with colour. Judith sighed deeply with content and went downstairs, looking in all the rooms as she went. The house was bigger than one would have supposed from the outside: too big just for her parents, she supposed, but they had bought it when they had married years ago and her father had been a partner in a firm of solicitors in Calne, and when he retired two years previously there had been no talk of moving to something smaller and more modern. Her mother had said that it would be nice to have enough room for Judith's children when she married, and meanwhile the extra bedrooms could be kept closed; if she was disappointed that they were still closed, she never mentioned it.

The weather was fine and warm. Judith shopped with her mother, helped her father in the garden and renewed her acquaintance with the large number of friends her parents had. The gentle, undemanding life did her good. Her pallor took on a faint tan and the slight hollows in her cheeks began to fill out. Before the first week was up she assured her mother that she felt fit for work again and played several vigorous games of tennis to prove it.

'You're not bored?' her mother asked anxiously. 'There's nothing to do except take Curtis for his walks and do the shopping and the garden, and you ought to be having fun at your age. We love having you, but what you need is a complete change of scene, darling.'

It was the next morning when the letter came from her father's brother, Uncle Tom. He had known about Judith's measles, naturally he had been told, since he was a doctor as well as her godfather. Now he wrote to ask if she could see her way to going to Hawkshead for a couple of weeks; his housekeeper had had to go home to look after her daughter's children while she was in hospital and he needed someone— perhaps Judith would be glad of an easy little job? keeping her hand in, so to speak. Two weeks would be enough, went on the letter persuasively, she could have the last week at home. There was a girl from the village to do the housework; all he wanted was someone to run the house, answer the telephone and do the shopping. Besides, he would like to see her again.

They read it in turns, and Judith had just got to the end of it when the telephone rang and Uncle Tom added his voice to the written word. Judith found herself agreeing to drive up that very day and stay for two weeks. 'Even if I leave in an hour,' she warned him, 'I shan't be with you much before supper time—I've only got the Fiat 600, you know.' She added: 'It will be more than an hour—I've got to pack and fill up . . .'

Uncle Tom dismissed this easily enough. 'Two hundred and fifty miles, more or less, even in that ridiculous little car of yours you should be here for high tea.' He chuckled richly. 'Do your best, girl, because I'm counting on you to get here.' He hung up on her.

'Well,' said Mrs Golightly triumphantly, 'isn't that exactly what I said?—that you needed a complete change? We're going to miss you, darling, but you'll be back for your last week, won't you? And Uncle Tom is such a good kind man, and a doctor too.' She added delicately: 'Is there anyone who might telephone or write to you? I mean, someone you'd want to know about?'

'No, Mother. Well, you might send on the letters, but if anyone rings just say I'm on holiday, will you?' She gave her parent a rather absentminded kiss and went upstairs to pack her bag.

Her father had fetched the Fiat from the garage tucked away behind the houses, her mother had cut sandwiches and filled a flask with coffee and they had both asked her if she had sufficient money. She hugged the pair of them; she would really much rather have stayed at home for the whole of the month, but perhaps she would enjoy the last week with them even more for having been away. She started off down the street as the church clock chimed eleven; Uncle Tom would have to wait for his high tea.

She went north from Lacock through Chippenham and then on to the M4 until it reached the M5, when she took the latter to

begin the long drive to the Lakes. The
motorway was monotonous; if she hadn't
been anxious to reach Hawkshead by early
evening, she might have chosen a different,
more interesting route. At the Birmingham
roundabout she switched to the M6 and
presently pulled in for petrol and sat in the
car, eating her sandwiches and drinking the
coffee, glad of a respite, watching with envy
the powerful cars tearing along the fast lane.
Once more on her way, pushing the little car
to its utmost, she thanked her stars that she
liked driving even at the sedate pace that
was the Fiat's best, otherwise the journey
would be an endless one. All the same she
heaved a sigh of relief as she left Preston
behind her and knew that her long day was
almost over. Once past Lancaster and
Carnford and she could look forward to
turning off the motorway at last.

The turn came finally and at the sight of a
small hotel standing by the quiet road, she
stopped the car and had tea, a delicious tea
with scones and sandwiches and little cakes,
all extra good after her long drive. She was

reluctant to leave, but the afternoon was almost over and she still had something under an hour's driving to do. But now the country was wide, almost empty of traffic, the mountains ahead looming over the fields and copses, golden in the sunshine. Judith went slowly through Kendal and out on to the Ambleside road. There was a ferry at Bowness, crossing Lake Windermere and shortening the road to Hawkshead, but she wasn't sure when it ran, so it was safer, if longer, to go round the head of the lake and take the road to Hawkshead. The village lay between Windermere and Coniston Water and had at its southernmost tip yet another lake, but a very small one, Esthwaite Water, and Judith slowed the car, for the country here was beautiful. Grizedale Forest lay ahead, beyond the village, and on either side of the green wooded valley were the mountains. The village lay snugly, a delightful maze of narrow streets and stone cottages. She remembered it with pleasure as she turned into one of its small squares and stopped before a house, larger than its neighbours with a flight of outdoor steps and small latticed windows. As she got out of the car one of these windows was flung open and her uncle's cheerful voice bade her go inside at once.

She had been before, of course; his voice came from the surgery, which meant that he would be unable to welcome her. She went through the half open door and along the stone-flagged passage to the door at the end and opened it. The kitchen, a good-sized low-ceilinged room, was not modern by glossy magazine standards, but fitted with an old-fashioned dresser, a well scrubbed table and Windsor chairs on either side of the Aga. Judith dumped her case on the floor, opened up the stove and put the already singing kettle to boil, for she wanted a cup of tea above everything else, and then went back down the passage and into the sitting room. Large, untidy and comfortable—no colour scheme, just a collection of easy chairs, tables, a fine old cupboard against one wall and rows of books filling the shelves against another wall. Judith opened the cupboard doors, collected china and a teapot, found a tray and took the lot back to the kitchen. She had her head in the pantry looking for something to eat when her uncle joined her.

He greeted her heartily and then studied her at leisure. 'Too thin,' he observed at length, 'too pale, too hollow-cheeked. A couple of weeks of good Cumbrian air and plenty of wholesome food will make all the difference.'

'That reminds me—I've put the kettle on. Have you had tea, Uncle Tom?'

'I was waiting for you, my dear.' His voice was guileless, his nice elderly craggy face beamed at her. 'And a nice meal after surgery, perhaps?'

'Seven o'clock do?' asked Judith, buttering bread, spreading jam and piling sandwiches on a plate. 'High tea, I suppose?'

Her uncle rubbed his hands together. 'Boiled eggs, and there's a nice ham Mrs Lockyer left in the larder . . .' He took the tea she offered him and began on the sandwiches.

'Did you have any lunch?' asked Judith.

'Coffee—or was it tea?—at the Gossards' farm—the old man has got a septic finger.'

Judith glanced at the clock. 'Surgery in ten minutes. Have another cup of tea while I change—the same room, is it? Then I'll give you a hand if you need one.'

She went upstairs to the room over the surgery, low-ceilinged and very clean with its old-fashioned brass bedstead, solid chest of drawers and dressing table. She opened the window wide and breathed the cool air with delight before opening her case and getting out a denim skirt and a cotton tee-shirt. She had travelled up in a linen suit and silk blouse, both of them quite unsuitable for the life she would be leading for the next week or two, and tied back her long hair with the first bit of ribbon which came to hand. She discarded her expensive high-heeled sandals too and scampered downstairs in a sensible flat-heeled pair which had seen better days.

It was a good thing she wasn't tired now,

for what with answering the telephone,
laying the table in the rather dark dining
room behind the surgery and going to the
door a dozen times, she was kept busy until
the last patient had gone, but once they had
had their meal and she had cleared away and
laid the table for breakfast she was more
than ready for bed. All the same, she stayed
up another half hour talking to her uncle
and before long found herself telling him
about Nigel. 'He's very persistent,' she
finished. 'I sometimes wonder if I should
marry him—I'm twenty-seven, you know,
Uncle Tom.'

'God bless my soul, are you really? You
wear very well, my dear. You're a very
pretty girl, you know.'

She went to bed soon afterwards, yawning
her head off but looking forward to her
visit. Her mother had been right, she had
needed a change; her mother had reiterated
her opinion when she had telephoned home
that evening, sounding triumphant. 'And
perhaps you'll meet some interesting
people,' she had ended hopefully, meaning

of course a young man ready and willing to fall in love with Judith and marry her.

Breakfast over the next morning and her uncle in his surgery, Judith left the girl who came daily to Hoover and polish and went along to the shops. She crossed Red Lion Square, passed the church and turned into one of the narrow streets, making for the butcher's. She didn't hurry, it was a glorious morning and the little cobbled squares glimpsed through low archways looked enchanting; she had forgotten just how lovely they were.

They all knew about her in the shop, of course. Uncle Tom or his housekeeper would have told them and news spread fast in such a small place. Shopping was a leisurely affair carried out in a friendly atmosphere and a good deal of curiosity. It was, the butcher pointed out, a good many years since Judith had been to visit her uncle, but no doubt she was a busy young lady and very successful by all accounts, although London didn't seem to be an ideal place in which to live. Several ladies in the shop added their very decided opinions to this, although two of them at least had never been farther from home than Carlisle. Judith went on her way presently, back in time to make coffee for her uncle before he started on his rounds and to help with the rest of the housework before starting on their midday dinner.

She pottered in the garden during the afternoon and gave a hand with the evening surgery before getting their meal. A busy day, she reflected as she made a salad, but yet there had been time to do everything without hurry, stop and talk, sit in the sun and do nothing ... hospital seemed very far away; another world, in fact.

It was on the third morning that Uncle Tom asked her to take some medicine and pills to one of the houses on the edge of the village. 'They're for Mrs Turner,' he told her. 'I could drop them off myself, but I'm not going to that end of the village this morning and she really ought to have them.' And as Judith took off her apron: 'Don't hurry back, my dear, it's a charming walk and such a lovely morning.'

The house stood well back from the lane, a few minutes' walk from the village's heart; grey stone and roomy under a tiled roof covered with moss. Uncle Tom had told her to go in by the back door and she walked round the side of the house, admiring the beautifully kept garden—Mrs Turner must be a splendid gardener—until she came to the kitchen door, a stout one standing a little open. No one answered her knock, so she went in and stood a minute wondering what to do. The kitchen was the best of both worlds: flagstone floor, a beamed ceiling, lattice windows and geraniums on the sills, and cunningly disguised behind solid oak doors and cupboards were all the modern equipages that any woman could want. Judith took an appreciative glance around her. 'Mrs Turner?' She called softly, and then a good deal louder: 'Mrs Turner?' And when no one answered said louder still: 'I've brought your medicine.'

The silence was profound, so she tried again. 'Mrs Turner, are you home?'

A door at the back of the kitchen was flung open with such violence that she jumped visibly, and a furious face, crowned by iron-grey hair, cropped short, appeared round its edge.

The voice belonging to the face was just as furious. 'Young woman, why are you here, disturbing the peace and quiet? Squawking like a hen?'

Judith gave him an icy stare. 'I am not squawking,' she pointed out coldly, 'and even if I were, it's entirely your own fault for not answering me when I first called.'

'It's not my business to answer doors.'

She studied the face—the rest of him was still behind the door. It had heavy-lidded eyes, an arrogant, high-bridged nose and a mouth set like a rat trap. She said coolly, 'I don't know what your business is, Mr Turner, but be good enough to give your wife these medicines when she returns. The instructions are on the labels.'

She walked to the door. 'You're a very ill-mannered man, Mr Turner. Good day to you!'

CHAPTER TWO

UNCLE Tom was in the surgery, sitting at his desk, searching for some paper or other and making the chaos there even more chaotic. Judith put down her basket and leaned comfortably over the back of a chair.

'I delivered Mrs Turner's bits and pieces,' she said. 'She wasn't home, so I gave them to her husband.'

Her uncle glanced up briefly. 'She's not married, my dear.'

'Then who's the ill-mannered monster who roared at me? He needs a lesson in manners!'

Uncle Tom paused in his quest for whatever it was he wanted. 'Charles Creswell—an eminent historian, highly esteemed by his colleagues, with a first-class brain—at present writing a book on twelfth century England with special reference to this area. I daresay you disturbed him . . .'

Judith snorted. 'He was insufferable! He ought to mind his manners!'

Her uncle peered at her over his spectacles. 'These scholarly men, my dear, should be allowed a certain amount of licence.'

'Why?' snapped Judith.

'You may indeed ask,' observed a voice from the window behind her. 'Tom, it's a waste of breath whitewashing my black nature—I see I'm damned for ever in this young lady's eyes. We haven't been introduced, by the way.'

He left the window and came in through the door, a very long lean man with wide shoulders.

Uncle Tom chuckled. 'My niece, Judith Golightly—Judith, this is Professor Charles Cresswell, eminent his . . .'

'You told me,' said Judith, and said, 'How do you do?' in a voice to freeze everything in the room solid.

Professor Cresswell lounged against the

wall, his hands in the pockets of his elderly slacks. 'I do very well, Miss Golightly. Of course my ego is badly damaged, but only briefly, I believe.' He spoke with a careless indifference which annoyed her as much as his temper had. 'Tom, if you're visiting up at the Manor would you mind making my excuses for tennis this afternoon? The phone's out of order . . . better still, I'll ring from here if I may.'

He stretched out a hand and lifted the receiver and sat himself down on the edge of the doctor's desk. He said softly: 'Miss Golightly, you really shouldn't slouch over that chair—you have a beautiful head and a splendid figure, and neither of them show to their best advantage if you will droop in that awkward manner.' He took no notice of her quick breath but dialled a number and started a conversation with somebody at the other end. Judith most regrettably put her tongue out at the back of his head and flounced out of the room. She was seething enough to scorch the floor under her feet.

The Professor finished his conversation and replaced the receiver.

'Married?' he asked casually. 'Engaged? Having a close relationship?—that's what they say these days, don't they? I seem to remember my granny calling it living in sin.'

Uncle Tom chuckled. 'Times change, Charles, and no, Judith is heartwhole and fancy free at the moment. Which is not to say that she hasn't been in and out of love, or fancied that she was, a great many times. She's a handsome girl and she meets young men enough at that hospital of hers.'

'And they fancy her, no doubt—let's hope that some day soon, she'll make one of them happy.' He wandered to the door, then said with some concern:

'She's not here permanently, is she?'

'No, no, two weeks only while Mrs Lockyer's away. And since she's not exactly taken to you, Charles, you needn't worry about meeting her.' The doctor's tone was dry, but his eyes twinkled.

'Thank God for that,' declared the Professor in a relieved voice.

At lunchtime Judith made no mention of the Professor, indeed, she talked animatedly about everyone and everything else, and when her uncle assured her that he had no calls to make that afternoon, and would be home to answer the telephone, she told him that she would take the Fiat and drive over to Coniston and look round the village and visit Ruskin's house there. ' "Mountains are the beginning and the end of all natural scenery," ' she quoted rather vaguely. 'I expect he was inspired by the view from his house.'

'And what about Wordsworth—only a step across the street to the school he attended, my dear, as well you know, not to mention the cottage where he lodged.'

'Oh, I haven't forgotten him, Uncle—only I thought a little drive round might be nice.'

'Of course, my dear. Why not go on to Rydal and take a look at Wordsworth's house? Although perhaps you might save that for another day.'

'Yes, I think I will.' For some reason she wanted to be out of the village away from the chance of meeting Professor Cresswell. She hoped most devoutly that he wasn't going to spoil her stay at Hawkshead, but if he really was writing a book perhaps he would stay in his house all day . . .

She set off after their lunch, going slowly, for it was but two miles to Coniston. Once there, she parked the car and set off for the John Ruskin Museum, then wandered off to inspect his grave in a corner of the churchyard, and then on to Brantwood to make a leisurely inspection of Ruskin's house. And after that she had to decide whether to have a cup of tea or drive on to Tarn Hows. She decided on the later, and was rewarded by the magnificent views of the mountains when she got there. She stopped the car for ten minutes and sat back, enjoying it all, and then drove on again, past white Cragge Gardens and through Clappergate and so back to

Hawkshead, just in nice time to get her uncle his tea.

Next week, she reflected as she boiled the kettle, she would go to Ferry Nab and across Lake Windermere to Bowness, and there was Hill Top, Beatrix Potter's home and Kendal . . . all easy runs in the Fiat, and if she had the chance, she could go walking—there were paths to the top of the Old Man, towering over Coniston, as well as less strenuous walks through the Grizedale Forest. It was a wonderful place for a holiday; it was a pity that Professor Cresswell's face, so heartily disliked, should interfere with her musings.

Not that she had much time to muse—Uncle Tom, called away to an emergency, left her to keep his evening patients happy until he returned, and by that time, there was little of the evening left.

The gentle routine of her days suited her very well; she was busy enough, but there was always time to stop and chat in the village shops, or spend half an hour with her uncle while he drank his coffee and checked his list of visits. It was several days later when he suggested that Judith might like to go to Kendal directly after breakfast. Mrs Lockyer went once a month, he explained, sometimes more often, and there were several things he wanted—books, a particular tobacco which the village didn't stock, and his whisky was getting low. Nothing loath, Judith agreed happily, made sure that things would go smoothly while she was away, made a neat list of things to be bought, and went to her room to put on something other than the denim skirt and blouse she had been wearing. She hadn't brought many clothes with her; she chose a silk shirtwaister in a pleasing shade of blue, brushed her hair smooth, found her handbag and went round the back to get the Fiat. She was in front of the house, with the engine running, waiting for Uncle Tom to give her some last-minute instructions about the books she was to fetch, when Professor Cresswell put his head through the window beside her.

Judith frowned. She hadn't met him since

their first encounter—well, church, of
course, but one couldn't count that. He had
been in a pew on the other side of the aisle
from Uncle Tom and her and she had been
careful not to look at him, but all the same
she had been very aware of him, for he sang
all the hymns in a loud, unselfconscious
baritone voice. And after church, by dint of
engaging old Mr Osborne the chemist in a
long-winded conversation she had been able
to avoid him.

'Going into Kendal?' he wanted to
know, without a good morning, and at her
frosty nod. 'Splendid, you can give me a
lift.'

'I'm going shopping—I'm not sure how
long I shall be there.'

It was a pity that Uncle Tom should
choose that moment to come out of the
house, exclaiming cheerfully: 'You'll be
back for lunch, won't you, Judith? I want to
go out to Lindsays' farm early this afternoon.' He glanced across at the Professor.
'Giving Charles a lift? In that case bring
him back for a sandwich.' He beamed across

the little car. 'Judith makes a splendid beef sandwich.'

'Thanks, Tom, but Mrs Turner's doing something she calls giving the house a good do and I can't possibly work until she subsides again.' He opened the Fiat's door and inserted himself into the seat beside Judith; the result was overcrowding but there was nothing to be done about that. She waved her uncle goodbye and drove off.

She had intended to go to Sawry and take the ferry to Bowness on the other side of Lake Windermere and then drive the eight or nine miles to Kendal. There would probably be delays on the ferry, although the season was only just beginning, but the alternative was a much longer drive round the head of the lake; besides, she particularly wanted to go that way and she saw no need to tell her unwanted passenger.

They drove in silence until they reached Sawry, and Judith instinctively slowed down, because it was here that Beatrix Potter had lived and she had promised herself a visit to Hill Top Farm before she went back home; if it had been anyone else with her, she would have had something to say about it, but the Professor hadn't uttered a word, which, she told herself was exactly as she wanted it. They drove on to Far Sawry and joined the short queue for the ferry and he still had said nothing at all, and the eight miles on the other side were just as silent. They were actually in Kendal before he spoke.

'Go through Highgate,' he told her. 'Into Stricklandgate—you can park the car there.'

And when she did, pulling up neatly in a half full car park, he opened his door and got out. 'I'll be here at twelve,' he told her, and stalked off, leaving her speechless with rage. 'Just as though I were the hired chauffeur!' she muttered. 'And why hasn't he got a car of his own, for heaven's sake?'

And he could have offered her a cup of coffee at the very least, not that she would have accepted it, but it would have given her pleasure to refuse him . . .

The town had changed since she had been there last, many years ago. The M6 had

taken all the traffic nowadays, leaving the
old town to its past glory. Judith pottered
round the shops, carefully ticking off her list
as she went, and when she came across a
pleasant little café, went in and had coffee,
and because she was feeling irritable, a
squashy cream cake. She felt better after
that and went in search of the books her
uncle had ordered, did a little shopping for
herself and made her way, deliberately late,
to the car.

The Professor was leaning against the car,
reading a book, outwardly at least in a good
frame of mind. Judith said flippantly:
'Finished your shopping?' and opened the
door and threw her parcels on to the back
seat.

'I never shop,' he assured her blandly. 'I
wanted to visit Holy Trinity Church, there
are some Megalithic stones in the vault I
wanted to examine.'

Judith had no idea what Megalithic
meant. 'Oh, really?' she said in a vague way,
and got into the car.

'You have no idea what I'm talking

about,' he sighed, 'Not my period, of course, but I felt the need of a little light relief.'

Judith turned a splutter of laughter into a cough. 'What from?' she asked.

'My studies.'

She gave him a sideways look. 'Surely, Professor, you stopped studying some years ago?'

'I'm a scholar, Miss Golightly, not a schoolboy. What an extraordinary name you have.' He added gently: 'And so unsuitable too.'

Judith clashed the gears. 'Don't ever ask me for a lift again!' she told him through clenched teeth.

They had to wait quite some time for the ferry, and Judith, determined not to let the wretched man annoy her, made polite conversation as they sat there until she was brought to an indignant stop by his impatient: 'Oh, Miss Golightly, do hold your tongue, I have a great deal to think about.'

So they didn't speak again, and when they

arrived at her uncle's house she got out of the car and went indoors, leaving him to follow if he pleased.

And if he does, she thought, I'll eat my lunch in the kitchen, and since she found him sitting in the dining room with Uncle Tom, drinking beer and smoking a pipe and listening with every sign of pleasure to his host's opinion of illuminated manuscripts of the twelfth century, that was exactly what she did.

Before he left he poked his head round the kitchen door. 'Your uncle is quite right, you make an excellent sandwich—you must both come to dinner with me one evening and sample Mrs Turner's cooking.'

Judith didn't stop washing up. 'That's very kind of you, Professor Cresswell, but I'm here to enjoy peace and quiet.'

'Oh, we'll make no noise, I promise you—I don't run to a Palm Court Orchestra.' He had gone before she could think up another excuse.

It was the next morning, just as she was back from the butchers with a foot or so of

the Cumberland sausage her uncle liked so
much, that he wandered into the kitchen
when surgery was over for the moment.

'No cooking for you this evening, my
dear—Charles has asked us to dinner.'

A surge of strong feeling swept over
Judith—annoyance, peevishness at being
taken unawares and perhaps a little excitement as well. She said immediately, 'Oh,
Uncle, you'll have to go without me—I've
got a headache.' She was coiling the sausage
into a bowl. 'I'll stay at home and go to bed
early.'

'Oh, that won't do at all.' Her uncle was
overriding her gently. 'I've just the thing to
cure that—by the evening you'll be feeling
fine again.' He bustled away and came back
with a pill she didn't need or want, but since
he was there watching her, she swallowed it.
'It's a splendid day,' he went on, 'so after
lunch I suggest that you get into the
hammock in the garden and have a nap.'

Which, later in the day, she found herself
doing, watched by Uncle Tom, looking
complacent. This reluctance to meet Charles

he considered a good sign, just as he was hopeful of Charles' deliberate rudeness to her. In all the years he had known him, he had never seen such an exhibition of ill manners towards a woman on the Professor's part. He knew all about his unfortunate love affair, but that was years ago now—since then he had treated the women who had crossed his path with a bland politeness and no warmth. But now this looked more promising, Uncle Tom decided; his niece, with her lovely face and strong splendid figure, had got under Charles' skin. He pottered off to his afternoon patients, very pleased with himself.

Much against her inclination, Judith slept, stretched out in the old fashioned hammock slung between the apple trees behind the house. She slept peacefully until the doctor's elderly Austin came to its spluttering halt before the house, and she just had time to run to the kitchen and put the kettle on for a cup of tea before he came into the house.

It would be nice, she thought, if they had

a frantically busy surgery that evening, even a dire emergency, which would prevent them from going to the Professor's house, but nothing like that happened. The surgery was shorter than usual; Uncle Tom put the telephone on to the answering service, told the local exchange to put through urgent calls to the Professor's house and indicated that he would be ready to leave within the next hour.

'And wear something pretty, my dear,' he warned her. 'There'll probably be one or two other people there—Charles doesn't entertain much, just once or twice a year—they're something of an event here.' He added by way of an explanation: 'Mrs Turner is an excellent cook.'

She was dressing entirely to please herself, Judith argued, putting on the Laura Ashley blouse, a confection of fine lawn, lace insertions and tiny tucks, and adding a thick silk skirt of swirling colours, her very best silk tights and a pair of wispy sandals which had cost her the earth. For the same reason, presumably, she took great pains

with her face and hair, informing Uncle
Tom, very tidy for once in a dark blue suit,
that she just happened to have the outfit
with her. Which was true enough, although
she hadn't expected to wear it.

They travelled in the doctor's car, driving
up to the house to find several other cars
already there. The house, Judith saw, now
that she was at its front, was a good deal
larger than she had supposed. It was typical
of the Lake District, whitewashed walls
under a slate roof, with a wing at the back
and a walled garden, full of roses now,
encircling it. She went inside with her uncle
into a square hall with four doors, all open.
There was a good deal of noise coming
through one of them; they paused long
enough to greet Mrs Turner and were
shown into a room on the left.

It was considerably larger than Judith had
imagined, running from the front of the
house to the back, where doors were open
into the garden; it was furnished with a
pleasing mixture of old, well cared for
pieces and comfortable chintz-covered

chairs. It was also quite full of people; women in pretty dresses, men in conventional dark suits. And the Professor, looking utterly different in a collar and tie and a suit of impeccable cut, advancing to meet them.

He clapped Uncle Tom on the shoulder, bade Judith a brisk good evening and introduced them round the room. Uncle Tom knew almost everyone there, of course, and presently, when the Professor had fetched them their drinks, he excused himself and left the doctor to make the introductions himself. Judith, making small talk with a youngish man who said that he was a cousin of the Professor's, took the opportunity to look round her. There were a dozen people, she judged, and only a few of them from Hawkshead itself. And all the women were pretty and smart and, for the most part, young. She thanked heaven silently that she had worn the silk outfit; it might not be as smart as some of the dresses there, but it stood up very nicely to competition. The cousin was joined by an elderly man whom she vaguely remembered she had seen in church; the local vet, he reminded her jovially, and pointed out his wife, talking to the Professor at the other end of the room. 'I've just given her a Border terrier and I daresay they're comparing notes.'

'Oh, has he got one?'

'Lord, yes, and a nice old Black labrador as well. They're in the garden, I expect, but they will roam in presently, I daresay—they have the run of the house.'

'I should have thought that having dogs would have been too much of a distraction for Professor Cresswell—he spends a great deal of time writing, doesn't he?'

'Yes, but he takes them out early in the morning before starting work—I believe they sit with him while he's actually at his desk, so they can't bother him much.' He smiled at her. 'How do you like this part of the country?'

The Professor's cousin had turned aside to speak to a young woman and presently joined them again, this time with his arm round the girl's shoulders. 'You have met?'

he wanted to know. 'Eileen Hunt, an old friend of the family.' He laughed. 'One might say, almost, very nearly one of the Cresswell family.'

The girl laughed too, and Judith smiled politely and wondered if they were on the point of getting engaged. She glanced down at the girl's left hand: there was a wedding ring but nothing else. Eileen caught her eye and smiled with a hint of malice. 'I'm not going to marry this wretch—he's got one wife already. You're not married, Judith?'

The malice was still there. 'No,' said Judith carefully. 'There always seems to be so many other things to do—I daresay I'll get round to it one day.'

It was a relief when Mrs Turner opened the door and, accompanied by the two dogs, marched across the room to where the Professor stood talking to a small group of people. Dinner, it appeared was ready.

The dining room, on the other side of the hall, was every bit as pleasant as the sitting room. Judith, sitting between the vet and a rather prosy elderly man who had little to say for himself, glanced round the big oval table. Eileen was sitting beside her host, leaning towards him with a laughing face and what Judith could only describe as a proprietorial air. Was that what the cousin had meant? Was the Professor going to take a wife? Judith felt the vague dislike she had had for the girl turn to something much stronger, which considering she didn't like Charles Cresswell one little bit seemed strange.

The prosy man, having delivered himself of a lengthy speech about local weather, applied himself to his soup, and Judith did the same. It was excellent, as was the salmon which followed it and the saddle of lamb which the Professor carved with precise speed. The prosy man seemed disinclined for conversation; she and the vet carried on a comfortable, desultory chat which took them through the delicious trifle and a glass of the Muscat which had followed the white Bordeaux and the claret, before the ladies rose from the table and trooped back into the sitting room.

'Very old-fashioned,' commented the vet's wife, 'but Charles is too old to change his ways, I suppose. Besides, I rather like it, don't you?' She tucked a friendly hand into Judith's arm and strolled to the still open doors. 'Nice, isn't it? Such quiet, and a heavenly view. We only get a chance to come here about twice a year, you know. Most of the time Charles shuts himself up and writes and the rest of the time he's travelling around looking for bits of mediaeval history. Your uncle tells me you're a nurse. That must be interesting.'

'Yes, it is, but I don't think I'll be able to bear London after this.'

'You live there?'

'I work there, my parents live in Lacock—that's in Wiltshire. It's lovely there too.'

Some of the older women joined them then, and the talk became general until the men came in and her uncle came over. 'Enjoying yourself, my dear?' he wanted to know. 'The headache's gone? Do you mind very much if we leave within the next few minutes? I've explained to Charles that I might get a call from the Lindsays later on this evening.'

He turned away to speak to one of the other men and Judith, finding herself with the prosy man again, listened with outward politeness and an inner peevishness to a lengthy diatribe against the local government. She would be glad to leave, she decided silently; she had no interest in Charles Cresswell or his house, or his friends. It crossed her mind at the same time that he hadn't any interest in her either. He hadn't spoken a word to her since his brief greeting; he had invited her out of politeness because Uncle Tom wouldn't have come without her, but he made no attempt to hide his dislike. And she disliked him too—heartily.

'A delightful evening,' she told her host as she and her uncle left a little later, and gave him a smile as insincere as her words. She was greatly put out at his laugh.

'Was it, Judith?' His voice was bland. 'Such a pity that you have to go back to

London so soon. You've had very little time to get to know us—you'll forget us, I'm sure.'

She said nothing to this but stood silently while Uncle Tom and his host arranged a date for a day's climbing. She would be gone by then, of course, but she doubted very much if she would have been included in Charles Cresswell's invitation.

They drove the short way back in silence and when she had seen to the small bedtime chores and left a thermos of hot coffee ready in case her uncle was called out during the night, she went up to bed. The evening hadn't been a success—but then, she argued with herself, she hadn't expected it to be. All the same, she was filled with disappointment that she couldn't account for. And she didn't like Eileen; she hoped she wouldn't have to meet her again, although that wasn't very likely. The girl lived in Windermere and she would take great care not to go there.

She went the very next day, much against her will. One of her uncle's patients, an elderly lady of an irascible nature, had driven over from Bowness to consult him. Her car was a vintage Austin and she drove badly. She had reversed into the doctor's stone wall and shaken up the old car's innards so badly that she had been forced to leave it at the village garage and then, considering herself very ill used, had demanded some kind of transport to take her home. It was a pity that Judith should go through the hall while she was making her needs known in no uncertain manner to Uncle Tom who, in what Judith considered to be a cowardly fashion, instantly suggested that his niece would be only too glad . . .

So Judith had ferried Mrs Grant back home, a pleasant house nearer Windermere than Bowness, and would have made her escape at once, only Mrs Grant remembered an important letter which simply had to go from the main post office in Windermere and would Judith be so kind . . .

She found the post office, posted the letter and remembered that she hadn't had her coffee, so she left the car parked and went to look for a café. There were any number, and she chose the Hideaway, largely because of its name, and the first person she saw as she went inside was Eileen Hunt.

It was impossible to pretend that she hadn't seen her, and when Eileen beckoned her over to share her table she went over, wishing she'd chosen any café but that one. But Eileen seemed pleased to see her. 'Such a pity you had to go early yesterday,' she observed with apparent friendliness, 'but I daresay you find our little dinner parties rather dull after London.'

'I don't go out a great deal—at least not to dinner parties. I found this one very pleasant.' Judith ordered her coffee and changed the subject. 'What a lovely morning.'

Eileen sipped coffee. 'Yes. I expect you go out a good deal with the doctors in the hospital, don't you?'

'Occasionally,' said Judith coolly.

'How romantic,' said Eileen, and flicked a quick glance at Judith. 'I daresay you'll marry one of them.'

Judith thought very briefly of Nigel. Her mother had forwarded two letters from him and she hadn't answered either of them; she went faintly pink with guilt and Eileen smiled. 'Wouldn't it be thrilling if he came all this way just to see you?'

'Very thrilling,' said Judith, refusing to be drawn. She finished her coffee. 'I must go—I hadn't intended coming out this morning and I've a mass of things to do. She smiled a polite goodbye, got to her feet and turned round, straight into Professor Cresswell. He sidestepped to avoid her and with a quick good morning, she went past him and out of the café. So much for those learned hours at his desk, brooding over the twelfth century! It rankled that he had found her visit to the house so disturbing— squawking like a hen, she remembered with fury—and yet he could spend the morning with that giggling idiot of an Eileen. Well, he'd got what he deserved, she told herself as she drove back to Hawkshead, and it was no business of hers, anyway. And in three days' time she would be going home.

On her last day, with Mrs Lockyer safely
back in the kitchen, Judith took herself off to
Coniston. She had promised herself that she
would climb the Old Man of Coniston, and
although it was well past lunchtime by the
time she got there there were several paths
which would take her to the top without the
need to hurry too much. She parked the car in
the village and started off. She enjoyed
walking, even uphill, and she was quite her
old self again by now, making an easy job of
the climb, and once at the top, perched on a
giant boulder to admire the enormous view. It
was warm now and presently she curled up
and closed her eyes. It would be nice to be at
home again, she thought sleepily, and there
was still a week before going back to
hospital—which reminded her of Nigel. She
dozed off, frowning.

She slept for half an hour or more and
woke with the sun warm on her face. She
didn't open her eyes at once, but lay there,
frowning again. Nigel was bad enough when
she was awake, but to dream of him too
was more than enough. She sighed and

opened her eyes slowly, and looked straight at Charles Cresswell, sitting on another boulder a foot or two away.

'Why were you frowning?' he wanted to know.

Judith sat up. Denim slacks and a T-shirt did nothing to detract from her beauty, nor did her tousled hair and her shiny face, warm from the sun still. She said crossly: 'How did you get here?'

'I walked.' He whistled softly and the Border terrier and the labrador appeared silently to sit beside him. 'The dogs like it here.'

Judith tugged at her T-shirt with a disarming unselfconsciousness. 'I must be getting back.' She got to her feet. 'Goodbye, Professor Cresswell.'

'Retreat, Judith?' His voice was smooth.

'Certainly not—I said I'd be back to give a hand at evening surgery.'

'You leave tomorrow?'

'Yes.' She started to walk past him and he put out a hand and caught her gently by the arm.

'There's plenty of time. I should like to know what you think of Hawkshead—of Cumbria—what you've seen of it?'

She tried to free her arm and was quite unable to do so. 'It's very beautiful. This is my third visit here, you know—I'm not a complete stranger to the Lakes . . .'

'You wouldn't like to live here?'

Just for a moment she forgot that she didn't like him overmuch. 'Oh, but I would,' and then sharply: 'Why do you ask?'

She was annoyed when he didn't answer, instead he observed in a silky voice which annoyed her very much: 'You would find it very tame after London.'

Eileen Hunt had said something very like that too; perhaps they had been discussing her. Judith said sharply: 'No, I wouldn't. And now if you'll let go of my arm, I should like to go.' She added stiffly: 'I shan't see you again, Professor Cresswell; I hope your book will be a success. It's been nice meeting you.' She uttered the lie so unconvincingly that he laughed out loud.

'Of course the book will be a success—my

books always are. And meeting you hasn't been nice at all, Judith Golightly.'

She patted the dogs' heads swiftly and went down the path without another word. She would have liked to have run, but that would have looked like retreat. She wasn't doing that, she told herself stoutly; she was getting away as quickly as possible from someone she couldn't stand the sight of.

CHAPTER THREE

JUDITH left Hawkshead with regret, aware that once she was away from it it would become a dream which would fade before the rush and bustle of hospital life; another world which wouldn't be quite real again until she went back once more. And if she ever did, of course, it would be London which wouldn't be real. Driving back towards the motorway and the south after bidding Uncle Tom a warm goodbye, she thought with irritation of London and her work, suddenly filled with longing to turn the Fiat and go straight back to Hawkshead and its peace and quiet. Even Charles Cresswell, mellowed by distance, seemed bearable. She found herself wondering what he was doing; sitting at his desk, she supposed, miles away in the twelfth century.

She was tooling along, well past

Lancaster, when a Ferrari Dino 308 passed
her on the fast lane. Charles Cresswell was
driving it—he lifted a hand in greeting as he
flashed past, leaving her gawping at its fast
disappearing elegance. What was he doing
on the M6, going south, she wondered, and
in such a car? A rich man's car too—even in
these days one could buy a modest house for
its price. And not at all the right transport
for a professor of Ancient History—it
should be something staid; a well polished
Rover, perhaps, or one of the bigger Fords.
She overtook an enormous bulk carrier with
some caution and urged the little Fiat to do
its best. There was no point in thinking any
more about it, though. She wasn't going to
see him again; she dismissed him firmly
from her mind and concentrated on getting
home.

It was after five o'clock as she drove
slowly through Lacock's main street and
then turned into the narrow road and pulled
up before her parents' house. She got out
with a great sigh of relief which changed
into a yelp of startled disbelief when she saw

the Ferrari parked a few yards ahead of her. It could belong to someone else, of course, but she had the horrid feeling that it didn't, and she was quite right. Her mother had opened the door and Judith, hugging and kissing her quickly, asked sharply: 'Whose car is that? The Ferrari—don't tell me that awful man's here . . .'

They were already in the little hall and the sitting room door was slightly open. The look on her mother's face was answer enough; there really was no need for Professor Cresswell to show his bland face round the door. He said smoothly: 'Don't worry, Judith, I'm on the point of leaving,' and before she could utter a word, he had taken a warmly polite leave of her mother, given her a brief expressionless nod, and gone. She watched him get into his car and drive away and it was her mother who broke the silence. 'Professor Cresswell kindly came out of his way to deliver a book your Uncle Tom forgot to give you for your father.' She sounded put out and puzzled, and Judith flung an arm round her shoulders.

'I'm sorry, Mother dear, but I was surprised. I had no idea that Professor Cresswell was leaving Hawkshead. I—I don't get on very well with him and it was such a relief to get away from him—and then I get out of the car and there he is!'

'You were rude,' observed Mrs Golightly. 'I thought he was charming.'

'Oh, pooh—if he wants to be, he can be much ruder than I was; we disliked each other on sight.' She frowned a little as she spoke because her words didn't ring quite true in her own ears, but the frown disappeared as Curtis came lumbering out of the sitting room to make much of her.

'Professor Cresswell liked Curtis,' observed Mrs Golightly. 'He has two dogs of his own . . .'

'Yes, I know—a Border terrier and a labrador. I've met them.'

'So you've been to his house?' Mrs Golightly's question was uttered with deceptive casualness.

'Only because I had to. Where's Father?'

'Playing bowls—he'll be sorry to have missed Professor Cresswell.'

'Well, he's got Uncle Tom's book. I'll get my case . . .'

'Tea's in the sitting room—I made a cup for the Professor . . .'

'Cresswell,' finished Judith snappishly, and then allowed her tongue to betray her. 'Where was he going, anyway?'

Her mother gave her a guileless look. 'I didn't ask,' she said, which was true but misleading.

There was a lot to talk about and it all had to be repeated when her father got home. It was surprising how often Charles Cresswell's name kept cropping up; Judith decided that her dislike of him had been so intense that it would take some time to get rid of his image. 'Hateful man!' she muttered as she unpacked. 'Thank heaven I'll never see him again!'

It was nice to be home; to take up the quiet round of unhurried chores, stop and chat in the village with her parents' friends, play tennis at the vicarage and take Curtis for the long ambling walks he loved. The week went too quickly and she found herself packing once more. The prospect of getting back into uniform held no pleasure, indeed she wondered if she really wanted to go back to Beck's. Somehow she felt vaguely dissatisfied with life, and Nigel would be waiting for her, he had told her that in the several letters he had written to her. He hadn't taken her refusal to marry him seriously; it seemed she would have to start all over again, trying to make him understand ... Perhaps that was why she was feeling so downcast. She finished her packing and since it was their last evening together, took her parents down to the Red Lion for dinner.

She left at the last possible moment the next day. She would go on duty at eight o'clock the next morning, but a couple of hours would be time enough in which to put her room to rights and get her uniform ready, so that it was already early evening when she drove the Fiat through the wide entrance of the hospital and parked it in the inner courtyard. It was broodingly warm still with the threat of a storm, and as she locked the car and picked up her case she tried not to think of the peace and quiet of Lacock. For some reason she did not allow herself to think about Hawkshead at all.

Beck's loomed all around her, an old hospital being modernised as fast as funds allowed, although nothing could eradicate its Victorian origins. The side door Judith went through still squeaked abominably and the serviceable brown lino on the passage floor was as shiny and slippery as it always was. Her charming nose wrinkled as it met the familiar smells, faint but unmistakable, of disinfectant, supper from the floor above her and the merest whiff of fragrance from the bowl of sweet peas the Warden of the nurses' home, a keen arranger of flowers, had set on a table at the end of the passage, by the door to the home. Judith had never minded the hospital atmosphere before, now suddenly she was assailed by such a longing to be in Charles Cresswell's garden, with its roses trailing over the house walls, scenting the air, that she could easily have burst into tears. She shook her head vigorously, told herself not to be a fool, and went through the door into the hall and began to climb the stairs to her room.

She hadn't finished her unpacking before the first of her friends joined her. Jenny Thorpe was the Accident Room Sister, younger than Judith, small and dainty and fair-haired. She made herself comfortable on Judith's bed and declared: 'How nice to have you back—you'll be on in the morning, I suppose, just to get the hang of things, and then go on duty in the evening? Well, it's busy, ducky. Miles and Reed have managed more or less, but no one replaced you, they made do with an extra staff nurse. Now tell me all about your holiday—you're looking terrific . . .'

She was interrupted by another girl with a round cheerful face and no looks to speak of. 'You're back,' she observed unnecessarily. 'They want you in the office right away, Judith, and I'll bet my month's salary that Sister Reed's gone off sick; I hear she was complaining all night about her feet.'

She was right. Judith was greeted by the Senior Nursing Officer with the brisk request that she should go on duty that very night. 'I don't know which way to turn,' declared that lady with an emotion she seldom displayed. 'Here's Sister Reed off sick and no one to relieve her and the surgical side so very busy. You will, of course, have an extra night off duty,' she added the ominous words, 'when it's convenient.'

Judith said: 'Yes, Miss Parkes,' in her calm way, well aware that no night was ever convenient. If ever there was a night when she could sit down and put her feet up for an hour, she would eat her very attractive frilled muslin cap!

There was just time to have a cup of tea before changing into uniform, finishing her unpacking and joining the rest of the night staff for breakfast. That she had had one breakfast already that day didn't deter her from eating scrambled eggs and toast and marmalade. She had been on the night staff for some time now and topsy-turvy meals when on duty seemed natural enough.

Ann Miles, the junior Sister, was already at the table when Judith got to the canteen, and uttered a sincere, 'Thank God!' when she saw her. 'I saw one of the surgical nurses as I came here,' she exclaimed. 'There's been an RTA, four injured so far and more in the Accident Room.' She added as an afterthought, 'Did you have a good leave?'

Lacock and Hawkshead seemed a long way away—a different world. 'Very nice, thank you,' said Judith. 'Tell me a bit more about this RTA.'

By midnight she was tired, but there was little chance to sit down even for ten minutes. The injured were all in need of skilled attention and as usual, she hadn't quite enough nurses on duty; she went from one bed to the other and then leaving Ann to cope, went off on her midnight round. She had seen Nigel, of course, but there had been no time to talk, and even if there had been, she was in no mood for personal matters.

She finished her rounds, went back to her office and sat down at last. There was a tray on the desk with a pot of tea and a plate of sandwiches, and she started on her scratch meal as she began on the paper work to be done before morning. Despite her tiredness she wrote quickly and accurately in her neat hand and she was almost finished, a sandwich half eaten, held poised, when the door opened and Nigel came in.

Judith looked up briefly. 'I'm busy,' she said, her mouth full, 'is it about a patient? That man with the shoulder wound . . .'

'They're all O.K. until Mr David sees them in the morning. I wanted to talk to you. You didn't answer any of my letters . . .'

Judith swallowed the last of her sandwiches. 'Not now, Nigel—I'm up to my eyes. I didn't expect to come on duty tonight and I'm tired.'

'Me too,' he yawned. 'What a life! If you

married me, of course, you could work a day shift or even do part-time.'

'Or stay at home and be a housewife,' murmured Judith, and drank her tea.

'Well, that would be silly. You're a good nurse and as strong as a horse, and the extra money would be useful. Once I could get a consultant's post you'd have to stop, of course, it would never do to have you working.'

She choked over her tea. 'Nigel, will you go away? I'm busy—I've said that once, and I'm not going to marry you—I've said that several times, and I mean it.'

Suddenly she couldn't bear him sitting there, looking smug and self-satisfied and not minding a bit about her tiredness. He'd be that kind of a husband, she guessed, always expecting her to be at his beck and call, ready to do what he wanted and never mind about her. She didn't hold with Women's Lib, but just at the moment she had a good deal of sympathy for the movement. She got to her feet. 'I'm going to relieve Ann,' she told him, and thought longingly of the tea still in the pot. 'Are you on call for the rest of the night or is Mr Wright?'

Nigel was still sitting looking sulky. 'Oh, Wright's on call if you should need anyone. What are you doing tomorrow?'

'Sleeping,' said Judith, and sailed away.

He hardly spoke to her for the next three nights and then luckily it was nights off for her. Tired though she was after a night which had stretched endlessly, she threw some clothes into an overnight bag, got into the Fiat, and drove down to Lacock. It took a long time because the summer holidays were in full spate, but to get home to a loving welcome, a hot bath, a delicious meal and finally her own bed was well worth it. She slept dreamlessly with Curtis spread over her feet and was up and dressed and making early morning tea well before eight o'clock.

Her mother, looking at her restored beauty, sighed, 'Darling, would it be a good idea to get a post on day duty somewhere? You looked so weary when you got home . . .'

Judith bit into toast. 'Well, I was. We've had a trying four nights, I daresay it'll be much easier when I get back—besides, Carole should be back, we've been working one short.'

'It would be nice if you got married,' said Mrs Golightly vaguely.

'First catch your man,' her father chuckled, and Judith laughed with him.

'I will when I find him,' she said.

It was wonderful what two days at home did for her. She went back to Beck's feeling capable of dealing with any number of patients, even coping with Nigel. 'I'll not be home next week,' she told her mother as she said goodbye. 'I thought I'd go and see Granny—she'll put me up for the night. I'm not sure which nights I can take off, so I'll have to telephone in a day or two.' She kissed her mother. 'I'd rather come home, but I daresay Granny wants a bit of a gossip.'

And as it turned out the next few nights held no dramatic upheavals. There were the usual admissions, of course, emergency cases in theatre, youths from rival gangs with broken bottle wounds, broken noses, fractured cheekbones, and besides these tiresome patients, some poor old soul beaten up for the sake of the few shillings they had. A sorry story, thought Judith, filling in her Night Casualty Book each morning, and not just once in a while, either. She was glad to be free at last and pack her bag again and get out the Fiat and make her way to St John's Wood where her grandmother lived in a pleasant little house with Molly, her housekeeper.

Old Mrs Golightly was in her early seventies, and still a spry old lady. She was small and thin, so that Judith towered over her, but although they were very different in appearance, they saw eye to eye about a great many things. She called now from the sitting room as Molly admitted Judith, bidding her to go in at once and have a glass of sherry before lunch.

Judith did so and was greeted by her grandmother, lovingly tart. 'Measles at your age!' she observed. 'How is it you never had them at the proper time? Lost some weight too, I see, though you don't look too bad, I must say. How is your Uncle Tom? It's time he paid me a visit.'

Judith bent to kiss her grandparent. 'He's very well, working much too hard; holidays just don't seem to matter to him.'

'Pour the sherry, child, and sit down—you can go up to your room later. Been up all night, I suppose?'

'Well, yes. But I'm wide awake at the moment, Granny.'

Mrs Golightly shook her head. 'It's not a natural life at all. Time you married, Judith. Surely to goodness you've met someone by now. How old are you? Twenty-seven? High time you settled down and had a family. I never did believe in women working.'

Judith sipped her sherry. There had never been any need for Granny to work. She had married young, slipping naturally enough into the roles of wife and mother, secure from every angle. Even now she lived in comfort with the faithful Molly and sufficient income to allow her the small luxuries of life. Judith sighed soundlessly. It wasn't quite the same nowadays—she would be expected to work, she supposed, at least for a year or so after marriage—everyone did nowadays. A home, she thought wistfully, and a husband who would work his fingers to the bone rather than let her work, even part-time, and children, growing up in a household where Mother was a permanent fixture. She shook the thought from her head. She was getting old-fashioned, the sherry was making her sentimental.

'I had a letter from your Uncle Tom,' her grandmother's brisk voice broke the small silence. 'He enjoyed having you, Judith—said you were a good girl and did a great deal of work. Said he wished he could have taken you out and about more; he seems to have plenty of friends too.'

'Yes, I met some of them.' For the life of her she couldn't stop herself telling her grandmother about the dinner party at Charles Cresswell's house, although she made up for that by saying: 'Of course, I didn't like him—intolerant and rude and arrogant; it's funny how you dislike some people on sight . . .'

'He disliked you too?'

'Oh, yes,' Judith put down her glass, 'he can't stand the sight of me.'

'How very fortunate that you are unlikely to see him again,' remarked her grandmother drily. 'He seems to have upset you a good deal.'

'Upset me? Of course not, Granny. Nigel's proposed again,' she added.

Old Mrs Golightly knew all about Nigel. 'You refused him, of course?'

'Yes, I—Granny, do you think I'm too fussy? Am I going to end up a dried-up old spinster?'

'No, my dear, you'll marry within the year, I have no doubt.' She nodded her head again. 'And not to that tiresome Nigel.'

Judith gave her an indulgent smile. Old ladies got fancies from time to time, and if it amused her grandmother to make arbitrary statements like that one, it did no harm.

She ate Molly's well cooked lunch with a

healthy appetite and then curled up in one of the large shabby chairs in the sitting-room. Her grandmother liked a nap in the afternoons, and there were several books which looked interesting. Judith opened the first of them and was asleep herself within two minutes.

Her two days went quickly although she did nothing much, content to potter in the tiny garden, do a few errands for her grandmother, change the library books and sit and gossip. It was on her last day that she saw an article about Charles Cresswell in a newspaper, lauding him to the skies for his scholarship and brilliant research. The book he was at present writing would be a world-wide success, it was predicted, and once it was published he was to embark upon a research into mediaeval manuscripts. He was, said the article, very modest about his work and disliked being interviewed—almost a recluse, stated the writer. Judith cast the paper from her with a snort of derision; what was so wonderful about twelfth-century England, anyway? And anyone who wanted to could go to the British Museum and look at dozens of manuscripts. The idea entered her head that she might do just that herself. She had an extra night due to her and Sister Read was back on duty. She began to work out the off duty in her head. There was no reason why she shouldn't add the extra day on to her usual nights off; it wasn't take-in week and anyway, each night was as busy as the last, so it would make no difference, for it would be inconvenient whichever she might choose. When she got back to the hospital she added one more night to her three off duty and since no one queried it, arranged to spend a day in London before driving home.

It would have been sensible to have gone to bed for a few hours when she got off duty, but for the moment at any rate she felt wide awake; besides, she would have a night's sleep before she drove home. She showered and changed into a cotton knitted dress and little jacket, made up her tired, beautiful face, piled her bright hair into a careless knot, found sandals and shoulder bag and went to queue for a bus. It was a pleasant change to feel free to do exactly what she liked with her day. Usually, if she went out in the mornings before going to bed, it was for necessary shopping or just for exercise. The bus was exasperatingly slow. She would walk back, she decided, but first of all, when she had spent an hour or two in the British Museum, she would have lunch somewhere.

She got out at last and crossed the courtyard, mounted the steps and went into the cool interior. It was ages since she had been there and she had forgotten how vast it was. She asked an attendant where the medieaval manuscripts were housed and wandered off in their general direction, wasting a good deal of time on the way, her attention caught by displays of pottery and jewellery, weapons and ancient stone statues. When she finally arrived she saw at a glance that what she had intended to be a casual hour or so glancing at twelfth-century relics was going to turn into an earnest study of several hours in length. She wasn't sure where to begin; the Magna Carta seemed a fair start, except that it wasn't twelfth-century. She hung over the glass case for a long time, trying to understand it, and then passed on the coins and seals. She was studying the Great Seal of Henry the Second when she felt that she was being watched. On the other side of the glass case was Charles Cresswell, looking at her with a nasty little smile on his handsome face. He said softly:

'Now I wonder why you're here, Judith Golightly? A genuine interest in the mediaeval? Or plain female curiosity about my work?'

She said with instant honesty. 'Curiosity mostly, but now I'm here interest too.'

He looked surprised and the smile disappeared. He said seriously: 'Why, I do believe you mean that.'

'Well, of course I do.' She turned away from him and became engrossed in a Saxon bucket with bronze bands, only to find that he was there beside her, pointing out the relief work on the bands, telling her the possible date where it was made and what it was used for.

'Very interesting,' said Judith, 'but don't let me keep you—I'm only browsing.'

'Then I shall browse with you.' No 'if I may', she thought crossly, and would have made a snappish retort, only he had already begun to lead the way to another section given over entirely to ecclesiastical objects. Indeed he took her arm and forced her to stop before a model of a twelfth-century church and began to point out its characteristics. 'A simple two-cell interior,' he told her, 'with an apse large enough to take the altar, slit windows, of course . . .' and when Judith asked: 'Why of course?' said impatiently: 'They were troubled times—and two doors in the north and south walls. From this grew the early medieval church. We can learn a great deal from the study of churches up and down the country—it's an absorbing topic . . .'

He had a pleasant deep voice, which combined with the hushed surroundings

and the relics of what must have been
another world had a soporific effect upon
Judith. His voice took on a dreamlike
quality, coming and going in waves, and she
was forced to keep her eyes very wide open
so that they shouldn't shut tight. She
managed that all right, but she couldn't for
the life of her stop a yawn; even smothered
with a hasty hand it was all too obvious.
Professor Cresswell paused in the middle of
a fluent description of animal and plant
symbols in churches and said in a quite
different voice, cold and silky and sneering:
'My apologies Miss Golightly—I bore you.'
He turned on his heel and walked away,
leaving her shocked into instant wake-
fulness.

She went and sat down on a hard wooden
bench against a wall after that. Her morning
was quite spoilt, she longed above all things
for a cup of coffee and bed. She closed her
eyes and dozed off.

She didn't sleep for long, and when she
woke, Charles Cresswell was sitting beside
her, reading *The Times*. She sat up with a

start and he said without looking up from his newspaper, 'You are a most abominable girl, you should have told me that you had been up all night.'

'Why?'

He ignored that. 'And why the British Museum? Hardly the place to visit with wits addled by lack of sleep!'

'My wits are not addled,' declared Judith, 'and I can see no reason why I should tell you anything.' She rather spoilt it by adding: 'I didn't know you were going to be here.'

'I'm surprised that you knew me—I had the impression at our last meeting that your greatest wish was to forget me as quickly as possible.'

'Well, actually it was, but I was curious about your work.'

He looked as though he was going to laugh. 'You're a very truthful girl, among other things.' He glanced at his watch. 'Shall we have lunch together? in a mutual dislike if you wish.' He smiled so disarmingly that she nodded, aware that she was hungry as well as tired.

'All right,' and then: 'That's twice,' she observed.

He knew what she meant. 'Yes, but the surroundings were pleasanter, were they not?'

'When I think about it it doesn't seem quite true. Are your dogs with you?'

'No—they're happy at Hawkshead and I'm never away for long.' He took her hand and pulled her gently to her feet. 'There's a small place near here, very quiet—no one will mind if you nod off over the soup.'

It was only a few minutes' walk and the fresh air revived her. They had a small table in the window, and without asking her he ordered an iced soft drink, enquired as to whether she disliked anything in particular and ordered for them both—iced melon, grilled sole and a salad and coffee. Judith was grateful that he didn't press her to have a drink. The food had revived her still further and she had better get back while she was feeling wide awake again. They sat over their coffee, talking amicably enough, indeed she found herself telling him all about her home, her pale face wistful so that he asked casually: 'Why do you stay at Beck's? I'm sure you have an excellent job there, but there must be other equally good posts.'

'I'm in a rut,' she told him. 'It needs something to dig me out—you know, something dramatic or urgent, so that I can resign without giving it a second thought.'

He eyed her thoughtfully. 'But preferably with a job to go to.'

'Oh, yes, I have to have a job.'

'Unless you get married?' His voice was casual.

An unwanted picture of Nigel floated before her eyes and she frowned. 'That's unlikely.'

He appeared to lose interest. 'Are you going back to Beck's? I'm going that way myself, I'll drop you off.'

Judith was too tired to refuse. He hailed a taxi and she got in thankfully and sat silently until it stopped at the hospital gates.

'Thank you for my lunch,' she told him politely. 'I hope your book is a great success,' she added for good measure, 'with rave notices. And please give Uncle Tom my love when you see him.' She sighed very softly. 'The roses in your garden are very lovely—I can't forget them.'

He got out and stood beside her, looking down at her sleepy face with no expression at all on his own. 'Quite lovely,' he said, and took the hand she held out.

'And I'm sorry about the yawn,' said Judith. 'As a matter of fact you were being very interesting. When I've had a good sleep, I expect I'll remember it all.'

'I shall remember too,' he told her gravely, a remark which popped into her head just as she was on the point of sleep and which she couldn't quite understand. She was too tired to bother anyway.

CHAPTER FOUR

JUDITH wasn't sure why she didn't tell her mother that she had had lunch with Charles Cresswell. On her next visit home she described her morning at the British Museum at some length, but left him out, and when Mrs Golightly asked where she had had her lunch, replied with limited truth that she had gone to some little place close to the Museum.

'Rather dull on your own,' observed her mother, who where Judith was concerned had a kind of second sight and felt that she was being put off. Judith agreed readily enough; it would have been very dull on her own. So with this her mother had to be content, though she did drag Professor Cresswell's name into the conversation from time to time in the hope that Judith might let slip some remark about him. She was a firm believer in romance, true love and living happily ever after, and it seemed to her that Judith and the Professor, once they had got over their dislike of each other, might make a delightful pair. Grand-children, thought Mrs Golightly happily, coming to visit her for the school holidays—something to look forward to. She found an article about the Professor in one of the loftier magazines and left it lying around, opened at the right page, and watched to see how Judith would react. Judith, a loving daughter but very well aware of her mother's wiles, ignored it.

She drove back to London under a sky heavy with the threat of a storm, but she was comfortably in her room, changing to go on duty, by the time it broke. It was still raging when she went along to take the report of the day's happenings in the Surgical Wing, with thunder crashing and rumbling and lightning streaking through the window as she sat down to the résumé left for her. The Ward Sisters would already have given their reports to the various night nurses on each ward and presently she would start on her round and read them all for herself, but now she digested the bones of the happenings on them, knowing that only the most serious of the cases would be in her own report. She had finished reading about the main wards and was beginning on the private patients' corridor when her eye caught a name. Cresswell—Lady Cresswell. Admitted with suspected leukaemia, aged sixty-one, living at an upper crust address in Belgravia; nearest relation: Professor Charles Cresswell. There were two telephone numbers, one a London number, the other, if her memory served her well, the number she dialled when she telephoned Uncle Tom. 'Oh, lord,' said Judith, 'of all the infuriating things to happen!' At least she was on night duty, which meant she would never see Charles Cresswell.

She started on her rounds, dismissing the matter from her mind for the time being. There was enough to attend to in the Men's Surgical ward where there had been four admissions, two of them in poor shape. Half way round, she stopped to have coffee with Sister Reed, compare notes, discuss the patients worrying them, and who was to do what during the night, and then she went on her way again. At least there weren't any theatre cases, which meant that Sister Reed was free to take over her share of the drug checking.

There were ten private rooms beyond the main women's surgical ward, lining one side of a wide corridor overlooking the inner courtyard of Beck's. They were pleasant, as pleasant as a hospital room could look, and had the added advantage of a separate entrance at the other end of the corridor so that visitors could come and go without disturbing the main wards. Judith dismissed the staff nurse who had accompanied her on her round so far; there was enough work to do without her keeping her unnecessarily, and the private patients sometimes took up a good deal of time—not being in the wards they had little idea of the constant round of chores going on, and while Judith found their leisurely attitude towards hospital routine irksome when she was busy, she hardly blamed them for it. After all, they were paying handsomely for their beds and treatment and for the most part they were pleasant, co-operative and grateful.

Of course, there was always the odd man out—and he was in the first room. She tapped on the door, and went in, sighing inwardly. Mr Forsythe had an ulcer, brought on by his obsession for making money. Even here in his hospital bed, he read the financial papers, spent hours telephoning those he employed to help him amass even more of it, and in between lived on stomach powders and a miserable steamed fish diet. No amount of arguing had made him agree to have an operation, and as far as she could see, they were stuck with him forever. She went over to the bed, wished him a cheerful good evening and listened patiently to his complaints. Most of them were to do with his stocks and shares going down instead of up, and any questions she might managed to put were impatiently waved aside. His ulcer was a nuisance, but quite secondary to his need to make more money. She coaxed him to take something to make him sleep and went on to the next patient.

Mr King, unlike his neighbour, had no interest in money, for he had very little of it, but he had a loving family who shared the burden of his hospital fees and brought him the cassettes of the classical music he loved so that he could play them incessantly, something he wouldn't have been able to do in the main wards. Judith listened to the last bit of Fauré's Requiem with deep satisfaction, offered necessary pills and went on her way, feeling sad. Mr King was a dear old man and wasn't going to get better. She knew that, so did his family, so did he, and there was very little to be done about it.

The next two rooms were empty, waiting for patients booked for the next day, and in the fifth room the young girl with the appendix was asleep.

The next three rooms were easy, all patients who were on the point of going home, merely wanting a few minutes' chat before settling down for the night, and the ninth was a young woman with a very small baby who had been operated upon for pyloric stenosis. The tenth door was shut, but there was a light over the door still. Judith tapped and went in.

Lady Cresswell was sitting up in bed, reading. Judith hadn't had any idea what she would be like, but she wasn't prepared for the comfortably plump, positively cosy figure leaning back against the pillows, who took off large, owl-like spectacles and beamed cheerfully at her from a round still pretty face, crowned by short white curls.

'Good evening, Sister,' she smiled, and held out a hand. 'I feel such a fraud, lying here, wasting everyone's time. I'm sure all these tests the doctors want to do could have been done at home . . .'

Judith smiled. 'Well, I suppose so, but it would have been a lot of extra work for them, you know. I see you're only here for a few days—I should enjoy them if you can, bed can be very nice when you're not ill.'

The little lady nodded her head vigorously. 'And I've a pile of books to read.'

Judith glanced at them, a catholic mixture she would dearly have loved to sit down and browse through. 'I'll change places,' she said flippantly because she sensed that Lady Cresswell intended to look on the bright side. She didn't know what her doctors had told her, probably a half truth, paving the way for bad news should the test prove conclusive. She was sure that her patient wasn't a woman to be fobbed off with vague talk, neither did she wish to be drowned in pessimism. They chatted happily enough for five minutes or so, during which time Lady Cresswell made no mention of her son at all. Perhaps they weren't very close, thought Judith, hurrying back to relieve Sister Reed; the bright little lady seemed quite the wrong type of mother for such a cold fish as the Professor.

She forgot all about it during the next hour or so, and when she did her second round, Lady Cresswell was sleeping like a child.

She was awake when Judith did her final early morning round, though; full of cheerful small talk, but Judith learned nothing of her personal life.

'You'll be having your first test this morning,' she told her. 'Nothing to worry about, though. I'll see you this evening.'

She went for a walk in the park before she went to bed; the storm had passed, but it was dull and oppressively warm still. There was really nothing to keep her from her bed and there was another busy night ahead of her. But in bed, she didn't sleep at once; she found herself wondering about Lady Cresswell. If they diagnosed leukaemia, whichever type it was, she had a good chance of being kept alive for a number of years still. Perhaps they would decide not to tell her; she went to sleep pondering the advantages and disadvantages of being told the truth or being fobbed off with a watered-down version of the diagnosis.

The first hour of the night went quickly. Judith was busy, but no more than usual, her rounds went without a hitch, and although Nigel appeared when she was barely half way round the main wards, she snubbed him so severely that he walked off, saying coldly over his shoulder that he wasn't on call anyway, and if she wanted help she should get Mr Wright or Mr Davies. 'I was hoping for a cup of coffee,' he observed frostily.

'Well, I often hope for it too,' said Judith, 'but I don't always get it.' She adjusted a drip to a nicety. 'But I daresay there's some on the stove in the Men's Surgical kitchen if you'd like to help yourself.'

He wouldn't, of course, he was a man who expected to have things handed to him and then cleared away afterwards.

It was earlier than usual by the time Judith tapped on Lady Cresswell's door and went in. Her patient was sitting up in bed looking charming in a pink bedjacket and discreet make-up, and sitting beside her was Charles Cresswell.

He got to his feet and wished her an unsmiling good evening, then walked over to the window and turned his back on them.

Judith flung a glance at his long lean back and then ignored him.

'Well, how did the tests go?' she asked cheerfully. The preliminary results of two of them were already in her report book, but she wanted to feel her way; perhaps Lady Cresswell hadn't been told the result, especially as they weren't conclusive. There was still a test meal to do, to eliminate a simple or pernicious anaemia and a sternal puncture.

'They say they won't know until tomorrow afternoon.' The blue eyes stared up at her as though trying to read her thoughts, so she smiled steadily back.

'It takes a bit of time—they weren't too bad, were they?'

'Good gracious, no, my dear. Tomorrow sounds much much worse.'

'Not really. They explained the test meal, I expect? I'll be along very early in the morning to get it started, you'll hardly be aware of it.'

'How comforting you are! But the other thing—I don't much like the sound of that.'

'Over in a jiffy, and done by your consultant's own hand. Nothing to worry about. Have you had your evening drink, Lady Cresswell?'

'Yes, dear. Something very nourishing and milky. And now before you go you must meet my son, Charles.'

He had turned round now, staring at her in a most unamiable manner.

'We've already met, Mother,' he spoke impatiently. 'In Cumbria.'

'Well, fancy that!' His mother looked from one to other of them in a speculative way. 'It is a small world, to be sure.'

Judith smiled in a non-committal fashion. 'Well, I must be going. I'll be along later to make sure you're asleep.'

'Yes, dear. What do you do now?'

'Well, there's still a patient in theatre and we're expecting two admissions as soon as X-ray has finished with them.'

'Good heavens! Don't you have a rest or a meal?'

'Oh, sometimes—it's not as bad as it

sounds.' She included them both in her smile. 'Goodnight.'

She left a silence behind her which Lady Cresswell finally broke. 'It's years since I've seen you to be the least bit interested in a girl, Charles.'

He put his hands in his pockets and looked down at his well polished shoes. 'I wasn't aware . . .' he began in a cool voice.

'No, dear, I daresay not. For a long time now you've treated all females in exactly the same way; pleasant, courteous, very mindful of their comfort and not caring a damn about any of them. But this magnificent creature seems to have got under your skin.' She put her head on one side and added thoughtfully: 'I wonder if she knows that?' And when he didn't answer: 'I was having a little gossip with the Day Sister this afternoon; there's a registrar very keen on this sweet creature—pesters her to marry him. He's a dreadful bore.'

Her son laughed. 'Mother, how uncharitable! He may be a very decent fellow.'

'He's very good-looking, so I'm told, and

very conceited—not her type. Charles, before you go—what is her name? She smiled gently. 'I know the Golightly bit—isn't that sweet—but the rest of it?'

'Judith.' He bent and kissed her. 'I'm going now and you're going to sleep. I'll be along tomorrow, probably in the afternoon.'

'Avoiding each other, are you?'

He shook his head at her. 'Dear Mother, quash your romantic thoughts, will you? I have no plans to marry, or for that matter, fall in love.'

'No, dear.' His mother sounded very meek. She was asleep when Judith did her midnight round and not a word was said about her son when the test meal was got under way in the morning. Having got it started, Judith left it to the night staff nurse and went to finish her report. Two more nights and she would go home again for her two days off. She tucked the pleasant thought away and bent to her writing.

That evening the report on Lady Cresswell wasn't so good. The red cell count was unsatisfactory and the white cell count was strongly indicative of leukaemia—not, it was thought, an acute type, which meant that with proper care and medication Lady Cresswell might live for a number of years yet. But there was still the sternal puncture result to wait for, and that would clinch the matter. Judith sighed, because she liked the little lady, and then because she had seventy-odd patients to think about as well, dismissed her from her mind for the time being.

Lady Cresswell had been crying, that was apparent to Judith the moment she opened the door of the room. It was equally apparent that her patient wouldn't thank her for remarking upon her puffy eyes and red nose, so she wished her a perfectly normal good evening, remarked on the beauty of an enormous bouquet of choice flowers on the bedside table and waited.

After a moment Lady Cresswell spoke, 'I insisted that they should tell me.' Her voice was small but defiant. 'They weren't going to, you know. They would have called it anaemia or something and advised me not to

get too tired and to eat liver. I loathe liver—
but now I'm not sure if I want to know after
all. Charles says it's a good thing because
now I can forget all about it and that I'll
probably outlive him, anyway.' She gave a
small sniff.

Good for Charles, thought Judith, and
said out loud, in a calm matter-of-fact way:
'He's absolutely right, you know.' She sat
down on the edge of the bed and took one of
Lady Cresswell's delicate little hands in her
own capable ones. 'If you were a child or
even a young adult, the outlook might not
be all that rosy, although they've got these
marvellous new drugs nowadays—but the
older one gets the longer you're able to
resist it—probably you'll live till you're
ninety-nine and die of old age! You'll get
your ups and downs, of course, but we all
get those, don't we? and providing you do
what your doctor suggests, you'll be perfectly O.K. And I've not made any of that
up, either—it's gospel truth.'

Lady Cresswell managed a quite cheerful
smile. 'What a nice girl you are, Judith! I

think I feel better already. I'm getting used to it, it's that that's so difficult, isn't it?' She paused. 'Tell me something—why am I in a surgical ward? I've only had tests done—they're not going to do anything they haven't told me about?'

'Good gracious, no! Didn't anyone tell you that the medical side was full up when you were admitted? Don't worry, no one's going to do anything. You'll be here for a few days yet while your treatment is worked out, then you'll be able to go home.'

'Charles won't hear of that—I've a flat here in London, you know. I'm most comfortable there and I have a splendid housekeeper, but he insists that I go and stay with him, at least for a month or so.'

'You'll like that. It's so beautiful in the Lakes—I'd live there if I could, and he has a lovely house. But you must have seen it.'

Lady Cresswell had turned her face a little away. 'Yes, dear,' she said vaguely, 'Charles and I spend quite a good bit of time together, that is when he's not writing.

He loved it as a small boy and his father left it to him—he doesn't care for London, but of course he has to come here from time to time.' She was silent for a few moments. 'You did mean what you said, didn't you?'

'Yes,' said Judith steadily, 'every word of it.' She got off the bed to check the charts. 'Would you like a mild sleeping pill, do you think? Or would you rather read for a while? I'll . . .'

The door opened and Charles Cresswell came in. He had a bottle under one arm, and was holding two glasses as well. He nodded to Judith in a careless way and said: 'I've brought my mother a nightcap—champagne. You'll have a glass with us?'

Judith paused half way to the door. 'How kind, but no, thank you.' She wanted to tell him not to stay too long, but one look at Lady Cresswell's face told her that champagne with her son at eleven o'clock at night was going to do more good than the most efficient of sleeping pills. She said merely: 'I'll be back later, Lady Cresswell,' in a tone of voice which implied that she hoped he would be gone by then, added a pleasant goodnight and left them together.

Lady Cresswell sipped her champagne. 'Charles, will you do something for me?'

He said yes without any hesitation at all.

'Will you arrange for Judith to come with me when I come to stay with you?'

'You would like that, my dear?' If she had hoped to surprise him, she hadn't succeeded.

'Very much. She gives me confidence, you see, and I—want that, just for a little while.'

'I understand. Yes, I'll arrange that, but you'll have to persuade her, you know. If I were to ask her she would refuse point blank.'

He spoke pleasantly with no sign of annoyance.

'You won't mind? Judith being in the house? Since you dislike each other, I mean.'

'Why should I? I shall be working for a good deal of the day—I've got the proofs to check, and I hope my manners are sufficiently good to get us through meals.'

His mother peeped at his expressionless face. 'Charles dear, if you hate the idea, I won't ask her . . .'

He put down his glass. 'Mother, I'm completely indifferent about the matter. It is, in fact, a good idea, because it will leave me free to work without delay and feeling guilty at leaving you on your own.'

His mother eyed him lovingly. He had lived alone far too long, in another few years he would be a dry-as-dust bachelor, sinking into premature middle age. Distinguished, good-looking, well-to-do, much sought after by women on the look-out for a husband, but quite impervious to them. Bother the creature! thought Lady Cresswell wrathfully, remembering the seventeen-year-old girl who had spent a summer charming the heart out of her son's body and then wafting away from him, swathed in white tulle and lace, down the aisle with his best friend. He'd got over it years ago, she was certain of that, although he had never realised it. She doubted very much if he remembered what the girl looked like. It was high time someone broke the spell, and who better than Judith with her lovely face ... she was a thoroughly nice girl too. She said soothingly: 'Yes, of course, dear. Will the hospital let her go?'

'If you can persuade her to come to Hawkshead with you, I'll see that there are no difficulties.'

And Lady Cresswell nodded happily. Charles had a way with him when he wanted something. She foresaw no trouble, and she was so determined to throw them together. She lightly dismissed the idea that neither of them might welcome the idea of being thrown—after all, she concluded inappropriately, love would find a way.

When her son got up to go presently, she offered a cheerful face for his kiss, assured him that she was no longer despairing and promised that she would sleep soundly. Which she did.

She had decided to say nothing to Judith in the morning; after a long night's work, she would be in no mood to be argued with or cajoled. Lady Cresswell possessed her soul in patience, forbore from saying a single word to her son when he came to see her, presented a bright face to the doctors and nurses and bided her time.

Judith was earlier than usual that evening. All three Sisters were on duty, which meant that the work load could be spread between them. It happened seldom, they would be back to their usual two on and one off on the following night, but by then her own nights off would be due. She worked her way round the women's surgical ward and started on the private patients' corridor, feeling a strange reluctance to get to Lady Cresswell's room. She hadn't expected to see Charles Cresswell and it had annoyed her so much that she had slept badly in consequence. But lightning never strikes twice in the same place, she told herself, it was just bad luck that he had come when she was there. All the same, she felt an unaccountable let down feeling when she found her patient alone. A very cheerful patient too.

'I've been waiting all day to talk to you,'

observed Lady Cresswell, 'I do hope you can spare me five minutes, Judith.'

'Well, as a matter of fact, I can. So far it's very quiet on the surgical side and I've got two other Sisters with me.' Judith smiled and sat down composedly by the bed. It took no longer to sit down and the patients relaxed more; hovering on one foot by the bed did no good at all.

'I'm going to ask you to do something for me,' began Lady Cresswell. 'You'll say "No" at once, but please, I do beg you, go away and think about it. It's very important to me, but I'm not going to fish for sympathy I have that already, I know that, but I know that I need help, just for a little while. I've remembered all you told me about living to a ripe old age, and I believe you, but I have been given a death sentence, haven't I? I'll accept that as best I can, but it takes a little swallowing. Judith, I want to take you with me to Hawkshead. It's asking a great deal of you—you've a splendid career here, and probably you've a young man here too—you're far too pretty not to have—and I've no right at all to ask you, but would you consider it?'

Judith sat and looked at her hands, lying quietly in her lap. Hawkshead, she thought, and all the glorious country round it. Uncle Tom to visit, the rose garden and last: Charles.

She raised her quiet face. 'I must think about it, Lady Cresswell, but I promise you that I will do just that. May I have a day before I give you my answer?'

Lady Cresswell managed not to grin from ear to ear. 'I understand, of course, dear. I'm to be here for another few days, I believe. I'm not sure how things can be arranged . . .'

'Or even if they can be arranged. It's rather unusual, you know. In fact I've never heard of it being done.'

Lady Cresswell looked faintly smug. 'Well, we can but try—that is if you agree?' She added: 'They tell me I shall grow no worse for some time, which is a comfort— several years, they mentioned. At my age that's very comforting.'

Judith had read the notes. Five years at the most, more probably two or three. And that with the very best of care and treatment. She said: 'That's splendid news! I may be wrong, but I think you'll find that after you've got over the shock, life will become quite normal again—several years can be anything up to twelve or fifteen.'

'You think so? Then I will too.' The little lady lay down in her bed and allowed herself to be tucked up. 'I shall sleep well, I always do,' she said happily: 'And you won't forget, will you, Judith?'

'No, of course not. Goodnight, Lady Cresswell.'

The rest of the night was quiet too. Judith had time to think, but by morning she had to admit that she had got nowhere at all. Oh, for a sign, she sighed as she started on her morning round. There was none, she had given her report to the Senior Nursing Officer and was making her slow way to breakfast when she came face to face with Charles Cresswell. Hardly the answer to a maiden's prayer but perhaps a way of making a decision.

His 'good morning' was perfunctory and he would have passed her on the stairs. Her weary brain wondered why he was there so early in the morning, but she couldn't be bothered to ask. She fetched up in front of him and said without preamble: 'Your mother has told you that she wants me to go to Hawkshead with her?'

'She has mentioned it.' He spoke carelessly and glanced at his watch, which sent her temper sky high. The effort to keep calm on an empty stomach and with the beginnings of a headache was enormous.

'It's kind of her to ask me, but of course I can't possibly do it . . .'

'Is the rut too deep, Judith? It's understandable, of course, you're secure and safe in it, aren't you; it leads predictably to steady promotion over the years, and a pension at the end too.' He ignored her angry gasp. 'Or Nigel, of course . . .'

'How do you know about Nigel?' she asked furiously.

His voice was silky. 'You forget that I spend a good deal of my life upon research work—I'm quite good at it.'

'You have no business to interfere!'

He raised his eyebrows. 'Who's interfering? Let me make it quite clear, Judith, that I am not interfering—I'm not interested enough. But let me also make it clear that I will do everything in my power to make the rest of my mother's life happy. Presumably you've read the reports. Even at their most optimistic, five years is a very short time in the end and in all probability it will be two or three, even less. There's no guarantee. And you did say that you were in a rut. Surely this is a heaven-sent chance to get out of it before you're too old.'

'I'm twenty-seven,' she snapped. Her blue eyes flashed and her pale sleepy face was pink with indignation.

'That's what I mean,' he said infuriatingly. 'I've never thought of you as a timid girl, Judith.' His mouth twitched at the corners and she supposed he was amused. 'You're still young enough to accept a challenge, you're strong and healthy—and with each year the rut's going to get deeper.' He grinned suddenly: 'There's always Nigel, of course.'

'How dare you!' she fumed at him. 'You're insufferable—just because you want your own way . . .'

'For my mother, Judith.'

She ignored that. 'Anyway, I can't leave at a moment's notice—I have to resign three months ahead.'

He examined the nails of one large, capable hand. 'Yes, I know that. There are exceptions.' He shot her a lightning glance. 'I'm on the Board of Governors, these things can be arranged.' He said in quite a different voice: 'Hawkshead, Judith, early on a summer morning, not a patient in sight, only roses and great sweeps of mountain and calm water—and you would be giving my mother a little longer to live because she trusts you and believes in you and you make her feel normal. Only one patient against eighty, but surely she has as much right to live as any of them?' He added: 'If you wish, I'll arrange things so that you can return here if and when my mother no longer needs you.'

He was cutting the ground from under her feet. 'I won't be rushed,' she said quickly, and he agreed at once.

'Of course not. Let Mother know this evening, if you feel you've had enough time to consider it.' Then he turned abruptly away from her. 'Good morning, Judith.'

Dismissed lightly like a naughty school-child, fumed Judith, racing down the rest of the stairs and catapulting into the canteen ten minutes late.

'And where have you been?' her friends wanted to know. 'You look as mad as fire, Judith—was it Nigel?'

'No, it wasn't.' She made an effort to be in good spirits. 'I've had a messy kind of morning, that's all.'

'Nigel's looking for you,' said someone on the other side of the table.

'Something wrong? That man in Surgical, the one with the hernia . . .?'

'No, silly, not patients. He's got tickets

for some show or other and he wants you to go with him on your night off. The tickets were given to him,' added the voice maliciously.

Judith was gobbling cornflakes. 'I'm going home. You go.'

'He's not my boy-friend.'

'He's not mine either.' She realised as she said it that he really wasn't, not even in a lukewarm way; she didn't mind if she didn't see him ever again, she didn't mind if she never saw Beck's again ... I must be mad, she told herself silently. I'll feel better when I've had a good sleep.

She buttered toast and had a third cup of tea; it was time she had some nights off, she was getting lightheaded.

CHAPTER FIVE

JUDITH knew what she was going to do the moment she opened her eyes that evening. She got up and dressed, went along for her breakfast and went on duty, and in due course reached Lady Cresswell's room. Charles Cresswell wasn't there, but she hadn't expected him to be; all the same she felt let down. She wished her patient a good evening, checked the charts, asked how she felt and only then said matter-of-factly: 'I'll come with you, Lady Cresswell, for as long as you should need me. There's one thing, though—Professor Cresswell and I don't get on at all well and I think that must be understood from the beginning. We both know it, of course, and I hope we're adult enough to be sensible about it, and I see no reason why we should have to see much of each other.'

'Charles has said much the same thing to me, Judith.' Lady Cresswell turned a beaming face to her. 'But as you say, you are neither of you childish about it. My dear, I can't begin to tell you how delighted I am! You're sure, aren't you?'

'Yes, I am. I think I've been wanting to get away from hospital life for quite a while, but I needed someone to give me a poke to get me started.'

'And I gave you that poke,' said Lady Cresswell with deep satisfaction. She closed her eyes and looked thoughtful. 'Such a lot of things to think about,' she remarked.

It was a little bewildering how quickly things were arranged. Judith had had no idea that one was able to leave one's employment with so little fuss or delay. True, the Principal Nursing Officer expressed regret at her going, but never once queried it. She had been told that she might go home in three days' time to visit her parents if she wished and then return to the hospital to collect her patient and be driven with her to Hawkshead. There was a chauffeur, it transpired, a steady reliable man called William guaranteed to get them there in comfort and safety. All this was arranged without a sign of Professor Cresswell, let alone anyone consulting her wishes. Once or twice she was sorely tempted to back down and refuse to go, and then the sight of Lady Cresswell's happy face made her change her mind. After all, one could not be so heartless as to cast a damper on what might be the last few months of her life. She bade her friends goodbye and listened to their astonished comments with a detached astonishment as great as their own. She must be mad, she told herself a dozen times as she drove herself home, and was astonished all over again at her mother's pleased acceptance of the situation.

'Nothing could be better,' declared her parent. 'Another year of hospital and you would have become so set in your ways . . . it would have been a job for life unless you'd married Nigel.'

Judith shuddered; Nigel had been tiresome. If only he had put his foot down and refused to hear of her leaving; declared that he loved her to distraction and married her out of hand—she might even have got to like him in time. He had done none of these things; he had blustered a good deal, but he had plainly been overawed by Professor Cresswell's power to get his own way. Judith had parted from him without regret but with the feeling that she had cut the last link with her past life. Starting again had its attractions, somewhat marred, though, by Professor Cresswell's dislike of her.

She spent two feverish days at home, packing clothes. It was high summer, but it could be chilly in Cumbria. She weeded out her wardrobe until she had slacks, cotton tops, cotton dresses and a thick cardigan, and just in case there should be any social activities, which she very much doubted, a couple of pretty crêpe dresses, a plastic mac, a pair of low-heeled worthy walking shoes, some frivolous sandals and a modicum of undies. She had no idea how long she would be with Lady Cresswell, but she doubted if they would stay there for more than a month, and when they did leave, she would just have to come home again and get warmer clothing.

Driving back to London, she reflected that her parents had been surprisingly calm about the whole business; after all, she was, from a practical point of view, being rather silly—giving up a good job with a certain secure future for something which might last only a few weeks, even months before she would have to find something else. Oh, well, it was too late now to worry about that. She was to be well paid and since there would be small opportunity of her spending any of her salary at Hawkshead she wouldn't be destitute. Besides, she had a small nest egg which she had prudently added to from time to time.

Her spirits lifted. It was very early in the morning and it was going to be a splendid day. The sun was already warm and the sky cloudless and the thought of being free— well, almost free—filled her with sudden pleasure.

She had arranged for one of her friends to borrow her car while she was away, a cunning move to ensure that it was taken care of and parked in comparative safety at the hospital. Lady Cresswell's old-fashioned Daimler was already parked at the entrance and a sturdy middle-aged man, whom she took to be the trustworthy William, was sitting at the wheel. He got out as she approached, took her case and overnight bag from her, greeted her civilly and expressed the hope that Lady Cresswell wasn't going to be too long in coming as the traffic was getting thicker every minute.

Judith took the hint and hurried up to the Surgical Private Wing where she found her patient dressed and almost ready but having second thoughts about which scarf she should wear with her elegant grey silk suit.

'The pink,' said Judith promptly, and to the little nurse who was in attendance, 'If you'll ring for the porter and a chair, Nurse, I'll go along and tell Sister we're ready to leave.'

'Lucky you,' declared that young lady

when Judith poked her head round the office door, 'off to heaven knows what fun and games while I'm stuck here for ever.'

'Well, there won't be fun and games,' observed Judith, 'and I daresay I'll be looking for another job in a few weeks' time.'

'Time enough to get our Charles in tow—we're going to miss him.'

'I haven't seen him for I don't know how long,' said Judith not quite truthfully, 'and he'll be buried in his books, I fancy I'm to be seen and not heard and make sure that his mother doesn't distract him.'

'It won't be his mother who distracts him,' her companion looked her over slowly. 'I hate to say it, Judith, but you look uncommonly pretty this morning. He's rather a charmer, you know.'

'Not my cup of tea,' said Judith lightly, not quite sure if she meant that or not. 'Are you coming to see us off the premises?'

She couldn't resist a quick look round her when she reached the entrance. She hadn't expected to see Charles Cresswell, but there was just the chance that he might have come to see them safely on the road to his home.

Lady Cresswell said quickly: 'No, dear, Charles isn't here. He went back last night.'

William, despite his stolid appearance, proved to be a fast driver once they were on the motorway; even so it was a journey of nearly three hundred miles and Judith wasn't surprised to hear that they were to spend a night on the way—a piece of news Charles Cresswell hadn't bothered to tell her, but then he had behaved in a very high-handed manner throughout the whole business and doubtless would again. There was no point in getting vexed about it, so she enquired placidly where they were to put up and was told that he had booked rooms for them at a hotel in Shifnal, north of Birmingham. They would leave the motorway to reach it, but it was a small elegant establishment, said Lady Cresswell, and quiet, in its own grounds.

With a stop for lunch, they reached the hotel in the late afternoon and Judith got her patient into bed without delay. Lady

Cresswell was happy and excited, but she was also tired. Judith stayed with her while she ate a light dinner, and then went down to the dining room herself, where the head waiter, quite taken with her pretty face, gave her one of the best tables and made sure that she lacked nothing. She ate a delicious meal, quite unconcerned by the admiring glances cast upon her from those around her. She was aware that she was beautiful; she would have been a fool if she hadn't known that, but she deplored her magnificent figure, considering herself far too generously built, even although she was tall with it, so that her vanity was small. She thanked the waiter nicely as she went, asked if she might have breakfast early in her room, and went back to Lady Cresswell, now ready to be settled for the night, but ready too for a cosy chat before she slept. It was almost an hour later by the time Judith went to her own room next door and another hour before she got into bed. She had meant to do some thinking, but she was asleep before she had even a vague thought in her head.

They reached Hawkshead in the late afternoon and Charles Cresswell, with Mrs Turner hovering behind him, was waiting for them. She had to admire the way in which he had everyone organised with the minimum of fuss and time. William dealt with their luggage, Mrs Turner bore the tea tray into the sitting room and relieved Judith of the impedimenta with which Lady Cresswell found it necessary to travel, and Charles Cresswell installed his mother in a high-backed chair while Judith poured her a cup of tea. Only then did he turn to her and ask formally if they had had a good journey.

'Excellent, thank you.' She handed him a cup of tea and poured one for herself.

'If you wish to telephone your parents, please do so—your uncle too.'

There was no warmth in his voice and she thanked him woodenly before addressing herself to Lady Cresswell's wants.

And after that she hardly spoke to him, let alone saw him for several days. True, he took lunch with them and if his mother stayed up for dinner shared that meal with them too, but if Lady Cresswell had a tray in bed, then Judith dined alone, for it was always on such a night that he was dining out, unable to leave his writing, or setting out on some errand which had to be done just as dinner was announced. Judith pretended to herself that she didn't mind; it was so obvious that he was avoiding her, and she told herself that she couldn't care less. All the same, she felt hurt and puzzled too, for why had he been so insistent about her accompanying his mother if he couldn't bear the sight of her?

The days wove themselves into a gentle pattern. Lady Cresswell didn't like to be roused until half past eight at the earliest, so Judith quickly formed the habit of getting up early, having tea with Mrs Turner in the kitchen and then pottering round the garden for an hour before she had her own breakfast—alone, of course; she had no idea where or when Charles Cresswell had his. She would have liked to have had it in the kitchen with Mrs Turner, but that lady didn't hold with that, so she ate it in lonely state in the dining room before going upstairs to wake Lady Cresswell.

The mornings were pleasant enough, and after the ordered rush of the hospital, very welcome. Lady Cresswell hadn't given in to her illness; her make-up was as faultless as it always had been, every hair was in place, every day time and thought was given as to what she should wear. Judith liked her for that and took pains to see that she looked as well turned out as possible, and on the days when Lady Cresswell wasn't feeling so well, Judith did her hair, helped her dress, and added a little colour to cheeks which were paler than they should have been. They sat in the garden after that, and if it wasn't warm enough, in the drawing room while Lady Cresswell worked at her tapestry and Judith knitted a sweater for her father and sometimes she would read aloud. It was all very peaceful and quiet and it might have been a little dull, but after lunch each day, when she had settled her patient for her nap, she was free for a couple of hours, and then she would go down to see Uncle Tom

or walk or climb a little. No one had
suggested that she should have a free day
and by the end of the second week she
decided to ask for one. A trip to Kendal
would be nice and there were one or two
things she needed. The butcher's son had
offered to drive her in on any day she chose
to name, and she would take him at his
word.

She was on her way to the dining room to
eat her dinner that evening when the
Professor came out of his study, looking
handsome and remote in a dinner jacket. He
would have passed her with a murmured
greeting, only she stopped in front of him so
that he had to come to a standstill.

'I won't keep you a minute,' said Judith
pleasantly, 'but I see you so seldom that I
must make the most of the opportunity . . .'

'Tomorrow morning?' he asked impatiently. 'I'm already late.'

'No, because tomorrow morning you
won't want to be disturbed, or you'll go out.
I don't expect you know it, but I'm entitled
to a day off—one a week at least—and I

should like one this week. Friday would do nicely if you could arrange to be at home with Lady Cresswell, or perhaps Mrs Turner could be with her?'

It was obvious that he hadn't given the matter a thought. He said stiffly: 'I'm sorry, I should have thought of it and made some arrangements. By all means have your day, and perhaps you'll be good enough to let me know at the beginning of each week which one you want. How long do you wish to be away? Perhaps I should warn the district nurse...'

'No need. I'll go after breakfast and be back by tea time.'

'You will be going with someone?' He spoke carelessly.

Judith thought of the butcher's son. George was a nice young man and there was no need to tell the Professor that she was going with him in the butcher's van. She told him yes, still very pleasant.

He nodded, glanced at his watch and said: 'If there's nothing further, Judith, I'll say goodnight,' and went.

She drank her excellent soup gloomily. It seemed very likely that he was rushing off to a date—that awful Eileen Hunt. There had been no sign of her yet, but Judith had been sent to the study by Lady Cresswell that morning when her son hadn't been there, to retrieve a letter she wanted to answer, and on the large cluttered desk there had been a large photograph of the girl with 'Always Yours' scrawled across one corner. Judith wondered if Lady Cresswell knew about her and if she liked the idea of having her for a daughter-in-law. It had seemed to Judith, studying the pretty, hard little face, that Eileen was the kind of girl who would arrange to have her mother-in-law admitted to a nursing home; it would be done very nicely and so swiftly that no one would notice or quite realise what was happening.

She ate the rest of her dinner with small appetite so that Mrs Turner wanted to know in some alarm if she was sickening for something.

After the first few days it was apparent

that Lady Cresswell hadn't taken any harm from her journey, so Judith suggested that the pair of them might take a short drive each day, after tea when Lady Cresswell was rested. There was another car in the garage beside the Ferrari Dino and the Range Rover, a Mini, not often used from the look of her. Judith cast an eye over the little car and went straight to the study, where, undeterred by Charles Cresswell's cold voice bidding her enter, she asked for the use of it. He hadn't answered her for a minute or two, eyeing her thoughtfully, then: 'Quite a good idea, Judith. I've wondered if I should have kept William here so that my mother could be driven round. By all means borrow the Mini—you will, of course, be careful . . .'

Judith drew a breath. 'You can always send for William,' she suggested sweetly.

'And if I think it advisable, I shall do so.' His voice was silky. 'And now, if you don't mind, I'm working.'

It was a pity, she thought as she shut the door with exaggerated quietness, that they couldn't speak to each other without being thoroughly unpleasant.

She took Lady Cresswell for a short drive that very evening. Someone had cleaned and polished the Mini and the tank was full; she really had to give the Professor full marks for getting things organised, but of course he was a good son, anxious to do everything possible to keep his mother happy.

They drove to Clappersgate, Skelworth Bridge and Coniston and then took the cross-country road back to Hawkshead, a successful little outing which she hoped would be the first of several.

Two days later she went to Kendal with George, sitting beside him in the butcher's van. They parted company in the car park with a mutual promise to meet at half past three and Judith wandered off to look at the shops, buy the odds and ends she needed, and give herself lunch.

George was already there when she got back, and she squeezed in beside him, rubbing shoulders with the Canterbury lamb and half pigs loaded into the back. She was busy removing a muslin-wrapped pig's trotter from the back of her neck when she glanced up and saw Charles Cresswell and Eileen Hunt watching her from the pavement. Eileen was frankly laughing; the Professor was inscrutable.

That evening at dinner, without referring to the butcher's van, he told her that in future she was to have the use of the Mini on her day off. He didn't wait for her thanks but made some remark to his mother, and as soon as the meal was finished he excused himself and shut himself in his study. He came out again as Judith was going to bed some hours later and very much to her surprise expressed the hope that she had enjoyed her free day. Moreover, his voice was kind and he smiled warmly at her.

She got up very early the next morning, prompted by the clear sky and the sunshine. The house was very quiet; she wrapped her dressing gown around her and crept downstairs. Mrs Turner wasn't down yet, and wouldn't be for another hour. Judith put on the kettle, opened the kitchen door and wandered out into the garden, sniffing at the cool breeze and the scent of the roses before going back indoors to make the tea. Too early to take Mrs Turner a cup and far too early to rouse Lady Cresswell. She took a mug from the dresser and carried the steaming brew on to the doorstep. Life was really rather splendid, she thought; Lady Cresswell was looking decidedly better—probably she had entered a period of recession which might last for weeks, if not months—the country around her was heavenly and it was going to be a lovely day, and over and above that, Charles had actually smiled at her! Quite carried away by her feelings, she began to hum softly and presently to sing, not very loudly at first, imagining herself to be Julie Andrews skipping over the mountains. She was a sentimental girl and the music seemed to suit her mood; for some reason she felt happy, although she really didn't know why. She sang a little louder; the bedrooms were on the other side of the house and no one would hear her. 'The hills are alive . . .' she was carolling happily.

'And if you don't stop that infernal racket this instant you'll be dead!'

Charles Cresswell stood in the kitchen doorway, looking murderous. He was still wearing the suit he had worn the evening before and it looked crumpled. He needed a shave too and his hair was standing up in spikes.

'Your room,' said Judith coldly, 'is on the other side of the house—you can't possibly have heard me.' She studied him for a moment. 'But of course, you've been up all night, living in the twelfth century.'

'The thirteenth,' he snapped, 'and how the hell am I to work? There's no peace in this house with you in it!'

She got to her feet, her splendid bosom heaving with indignation and, although she didn't recognise it as such, unhappiness. 'In that case——' she began haughtily.

'Don't be a fool,' he begged her. 'Wallowing in hurt pride just because I uttered a mild reproof—and God knows I have good reason—all that sentimental nonsense about the hills being alive!'

She interrupted him fiercely. 'But they are, they are—when you're happy and content and the sun is shining. But how would you know about that? You're not alive, you're buried in the twelfth century,' she corrected herself—'well, the thirteenth, surrounded by dusty old books and papers shouting at people when they disturb your train of thought.' She slammed down her mug. 'Bah!' she said grandly, and swept past him into the hall and up the stairs.

Mrs Turner was coming down the stairs. 'Do I hear you having words with the Professor?' she asked in a soothing, motherly voice as she came abreast of Judith. 'A nasty temper when he's roused, has our Mr Charles. Don't you take any notice, dearie, he'll be sweeter when he's had his breakfast.

Judith muttered and ran on up to her room. Nothing would sweeten Charles Cresswell, he was sour, rude and quite impossible. Let him eat his breakfast alone, she'd choke if she had to share it with him!

She heard him come upstairs presently

and go along to his room. She dressed quickly and crept down to lay a tray for herself under Mrs Turner's sympathetic eye. 'A nice pot of tea, Miss Judith,' coaxed that lady, 'and there's a lovely brown egg just waiting to be boiled, you've plenty of time to eat it before you see to Lady Cresswell. Why not take the tray up the garden? There's that nice quiet corner behind the summerhouse . . .'

Judith gave her a quick hug, agreed that it was a splendid idea and bore her breakfast along the brick path between the roses, to perch on the small stone seat snugly built into the corner hedge and demolish the brown egg, a large amount of bread and butter and several cups of tea. She was almost finished when the Professor stuck his head round the corner of the summer house. 'Hiding?' he wanted to know, nastily.

'Certainly not. I like to eat breakfast out of doors.'

'And not share it with an ill-tempered historian who's never civil?'

'You said that,' she pointed out sweetly,

'not I,' and glanced at him, to see an expression on his face which puzzled her. Regret? Disappointment? Sad resignation? It might be any of those on anyone else, but certainly not on his handsome features.

He said evenly, 'It will suit me better if I breakfast in my study—it will be less of an interruption to my work.'

He had gone before Judith could reply, and presently she went back to the house to take up Lady Cresswell's breakfast tray and start off on the leisurely business of getting her patient ready to face another day. It was after she had done this and gone off to the village on an errand and to have ten minutes' chat with Uncle Tom that Charles joined his mother under the beech tree in the garden.

'I've been on the phone to Dr Thorpe,' he told her. 'He's very pleased with the latest tests and thinks that this is a period of recession—possibly a lengthy one. That's splendid news, my dear, and I'm wondering if it gives you the confidence to enjoy a change of scene? I don't have to tell you that

I enjoy having you here, but a few weeks' warm sunshine before the colder weather might do you good . . .'

'I'm preventing you from working, Charles?'

He smiled at her. 'No, Mother.'

'But Judith is?'

She asked the question quietly and he didn't answer her, staring away over her head. 'Shall I get another nurse?'

He said instantly: 'No. She's a splendid nurse and companion for you and I trust her.' He smiled again, rather bitterly. 'I find her—er—disturbing—larger than life . . .'

His mother nodded, taking care not to smile. 'A big girl,' she offered, 'what your father would have called a fine figure of a woman.' There was a pause until she went on easily: 'I know where I should like to go. Do you remember our holidays in the Algarve? Before you were born we used to go there too, at the foot of those mountains— the Monchiques. I'd like to go there again, Charles. Could you find us a villa somewhere between Silves and Monchique village? For three weeks or a month?'

'It will still be very warm . . .'

'You forget we shall be near the mountains and much cooler. We shall want a swimming pool, of course, and a housekeeper and a gardener who can drive.'

'You would really like that?'

'Yes, dear. Will you see to everything? I'd like to go as soon as possible, while I'm feeling so well—shall we say a month? That should give you time.'

'Time for what, Mother?' He was looking very intently at her.

'Oh, to get your research done, Charles.' Lady Cresswell raised innocent blue eyes to his, and he smiled faintly, this time with amusement.

'I'll see about it right away. Will you tell Judith?'

And when Judith got back she was told—in a vague roundabout fashion and given no chance to say much, because Lady Cresswell launched into a rambling discussion as to ways and means; clothes, passports and whether Judith would like to go home for a day or two before they went? She had no clear answers to any of the questions Judith put to her, it was Charles Cresswell, coming in during a more than long-winded reminiscence of his mother's, who settled everything with a few words. He would be going to London on the following day, he would collect his mother's passport and anything else she might need if she would make out a list. 'And you?' he asked Judith, who was still getting used to the idea. 'Do you need anything?'

'My passport, my clothes—they're at home.' She didn't add any more—let him worry about how she was to get them, since he was the one responsible for the sudden upheaval.

'Give me a letter for your mother and I'll bring what you need back with me. You may like to telephone her.'

She thanked him calmly; there was no point in arguing. It would get her nowhere, nor had she any reason to be grateful for his offer. She had been bustled into the whole thing with no vestige of consideration just because it suited him. When she had a chance she would tell him so.

She had no chance; he left early the next morning, telephoned his mother the following day to say that he had rented a villa just outside Silves for three weeks, and told her that he would return late on the following day.

Judith, informed of this by Lady Cresswell, marvelled at the speed with which everything was being arranged. She supposed that knowing the right people and having the money to get what one wanted must help, plus his desire to get rid of her as soon as possible, because in the light of their unfriendly encounters, that must be the strong reason spurring him on. Indeed, she was so sure of this that she had suggested to Lady Cresswell that she might like to engage another nurse, only to be met with a tearful demand as to whether she wasn't happy, or being paid enough or was bored to death, mewed up all day with an old woman. She had hastily rescinded her suggestion and had spent the rest of the evening coaxing her patient into a happy frame of mind again.

She lay thinking about it after she had gone to bed; away from the Professor probably she would be much happier; somehow he cast such a gloom over everything—she supposed that was why she felt vaguely unhappy. Before she fell asleep she heard the car and presently his quiet tread in the house. He didn't come upstairs immediately, and she was asleep long before he did.

They set out a few days later. Judith had been a little surprised at her parents' pleasure at her going; it was obvious to her that Charles Cresswell had presented them with the charming side of his character when he had gone to her home to fetch her things and they were wholehearted in their approbation of him. Her mother's letter had been full of enthusiasm about the whole thing and had taken it for granted that Judith was just as enthusiastic. And so had Uncle Tom.

She had spent a busy day or two packing for both of them, and when the Professor, after half an hour's talk with his mother, had got into his car and driven away on the evening previous to their departure, she hadn't been surprised. He had given her a list of things to do and remember: the local doctor, the local hospital, the bank she should go to when they needed money, the names of the housekeeper and her husband, the gardener chauffeur, telephone numbers where he himself could be reached if necessary—even the current rate of exchange—there was even a substantial sum of money to cover expenses. But he hadn't wished her goodbye.

William had arrived the night before to drive them to Manchester Airport so that their journey there was effortless. Lady Cresswell was excited and talked incessantly, and once or twice Judith caught a smug expression on her face and wondered why.

She found out soon enough. Charles was waiting for them at the airport and she realised with a mixture of pleasure and annoyance that he was travelling with them; indeed, her tongue betrayed her into asking: 'You're coming too, Professor?' In a voice which sounded far from pleased.

His smile was thin. 'Don't worry, Judith, I shall see you safely into the villa and then return home—a matter of a day or two.'

She went pink under his amused eyes.

They travelled in comfort, first class, of course, and by the time she had settled Lady Cresswell, found the book she wanted to read, provided her with her handbag and the barley sugar she was sure would overcome any tendency to sickness, they were airborne. Judith, sitting on the opposite side to mother and son, peered out of the window, watching houses and fields and villages getting smaller and smaller until the air hostess came with their lunch. When she looked again they were over water and presently crossing northern France. There was cloud after that as they crossed the Bay of Biscay, so she sat back quietly, reviewing the next few weeks, making sure that she understood her instructions. She had

brought a phrase book with her; she opened
it now and struggled with a few everyday
words. Lady Cresswell spoke a little Portuguese, but she wouldn't always be there.
It looked to be a difficult language, perhaps
she would pick it up more quickly once they
were there. She closed her eyes and dozed
until a voice advised her to fasten her seat
belt.

They were out of the cloud now and the
sea and coastline lay below. It looked very
different from England, even the earth was a
bright terra cotta and there were a great
many trees. They would be passing over the
mountains which separated Algarve from
the neighbouring province, and Lady Cresswell leaned across to say: 'That's where
we're going, Judith—it's beautiful, and did
you ever see such a lovely blue sky? I can't
wait!'

The Professor had his handsome nose
buried in a book, but he lowered it now with
an air of resignation as the plane slid
smoothly over the coast, circling over the
golden sand below to make it's final run in.

The airport at Faro was a small one and the formalities brief. He ushered them both towards the entrance where a man met them with wide smiles. Judith wondered idly how Charles had contrived to have everything so smoothly arranged in so short a time. Probably he was an old hand at the game; he didn't appear to be the kind of man to travel in even the smallest discomfort, and to give him his due, he would take care that his mother had no delays or discomfort either. Judith smiled at the driver as he ushered them to the car and he smiled even more broadly. She hoped she would be able to sit in front with him; he looked friendly and the Professor looked even more unfriendly than usual.

She was doomed to disappointment. The two men held a brief conversation, then Charles helped his mother into the back seat, invited Judith to join her and got behind the wheel himself.

'I shall have a nap,' declared Lady Cresswell, 'but I want you to wake me when we get to the hill above Silves, dear.'

Which left Judith sitting behind a silent Professor, looking at all the strange sights around her and not daring to ask him about them.

A bad start, but perhaps it would be better when he'd gone back home.

CHAPTER SIX

THERE was such a lot to see. It was the hottest part of the day and the whitewashed houses with their red-tiled roofs looked brilliant against the vivid blue sky. They had taken the coast road, going west away from Faro, and once clear of the town they saw that it was bordered by orange and lemon trees, fig trees and almond trees and geometrically neat rows of vines, and every few miles a village dominated by a whitewashed church, its small houses shuttered against the sun, dogs lying in the shade and almost no one to be seen. And flowers— flowers everywhere.

The Professor drove fast, seemingly as much at home on the opposite side of the road as the local inhabitants. He had taken his jacket off and was in his shirtsleeves, and for all the notice he took of Judith he might

have been alone. She gazed out at the
strangeness of it all, longing to ask why the
chimneypots looked like miniature minarets,
why there were no cows, why the village
shops looked like dim caves ... Lady
Cresswell was asleep, so there was no one to
ask. She contained her impatience, watching
for signposts and the names of the villages
they passed through.

There was a glimpse of the sea from time
to time, but presently they took a right-hand
fork in the road which was signposted Silves
and drove along steadily rising ground, well
surfaced but narrow. Indeed, the oncoming
traffic passed them with inches to spare, and
without slackening its speed. Charles Cresswell didn't slacken his speed either, nor did
he seem in the least discomposed. Judith,
who had been getting a little tense, allowed
herself to relax and turned her attention to
the scenery once more.

There were some splendid villas, she
noticed, with magnificent grounds and a
glimpse of swimming pools, a contrast to
the small box-like flat-roofed houses lining

the village streets, but although there might be poverty she could see no squalor, and the sunshine and the warmth were kind to even the dullest of them. They reached the crown of a hill and there before them was Silves, lying cradled in the hills, overshadowed by its ruined castle and the white-walled cathedral. Charles Cresswell drew into the side of the road and looked over his shoulder. 'My mother wanted to be wakened,' he reminded Judith.

Lady Cresswell opened her eyes at once and said like a child: 'Oh, it's hardly changed. Don't you find it charming, Judith? And this is the best view of the town. Charles, I want to stop just for a minute. You can drive up to the cathedral, can't you, and turn?'

It did look charming, thought Judith, with its white houses clustered under the blue sky. She asked: 'How old is the castle?'

'Moorish,' said the Professor at once. 'It had a very interesting history—the cathedral is built on the foundations of a mosque. It's a little disappointing inside, but well worth a visit—in any case, I doubt if you'll find much to engage your interest.'

'Why not?'

'I'm under the impression that you find ancient history boring.' He sounded so bland that she longed to hit him.

'It rather depends on who's telling me about it,' she told him. She found his soft laugh very irritating.

They drove on presently, down the hill and then along the road curving to the town's centre and then up the hill towards the castle, but Lady Cresswell didn't get out, only sat looking round her. They went back down the hill then and out of the sleepy little town, past a handful of shops and a mixture of tiny square houses and modern villas, until the last of the houses dwindled away and only the villas, getting more and more splendid as they climbed, remained. The mountains were much nearer now and Lady Cresswell observed excitedly: 'We must be nearly there—you did say it was before we reached Caldas, didn't you, Charles?' She turned to Judith. 'Caldas is a spa—a very small one—just off the main road to Monchique village. We'll go there one day—one has to drink the waters, of course, but there is, or there was, a small restaurant there. There's a hospital there too,' she added.

'For the spa patients,' observed Judith briskly. 'I expect the water tastes foul, but it would be fun to go, wouldn't it, and Monchique—is that larger than Silves?'

It was Charles who answered her. 'No, it's fairly high up in the mountains, magnificent scenery and that's about all.'

He had slowed the car and now turned off the road, going up a dirt track through orange trees merging into the forest on the lower slopes of the mountains. The track ended in a pair of gates, standing open, and beyond a short drive leading to an elegant villa, white-walled and red-roofed like every other house, but with a terrace and a verandah and wrought iron balconies. The front door was solid and carved, and was opened as they reached it by a small thin dark woman, dressed entirely in black, who

greeted them unsmilingly and stood aside
for them to go in. The hall was large and
cool and dim with doors on all sides, and an
open archway leading to a lofty room with
windows on two sides, its tiled floors strewn
with rugs and comfortable chairs scattered
round. There was an open fireplace in one
corner, crowned by a great hood, and
tapestries on the walls. A rather lovely
room, thought Judith, and very different
from home.

The Professor spoke to the woman as
they went in, and a tiny bit of Judith's
mind registered the fact that he spoke
Portuguese. Clever Dick, she thought
crossly, trust him to be perfect, not for
him sign language and speaking English
rather more loudly than usual, which was
what she'd have to do . . .

She settled his mother in a chair and as
the woman reappeared with a tea tray, drew
a small table beside it. 'This is Teresa,'
observed Charles Cresswell. 'She and her
husband Augusto will be looking after you.
A girl will come each day to help with the

cleaning and to see to the laundry and so on.' He glanced at Judith. 'You have all the information you're likely to need, if there's anything else, I shall be here for the next two days.'

Judith said blankly: 'Oh, will you?' and he laughed. She looked away, colouring faintly because it was quite clear that he had read her thoughts.

They went upstairs to their rooms after tea, large airy apartments at the front of the villa with a communicating door, and opening out on to a shaded balcony. It gave a splendid view of the garden and surrounding countryside, heavily wooded with cork trees merging into orderly rows of orange trees. The garden was lovely, a riot of roses and summer flowers and close to the house a swimming pool. Judith gave a sigh of pleasure and went to unpack for her patient and settle her down for a nap on the chaise-longue at the open window.

Lady Cresswell was tired but happy.

'How about dinner in bed?' suggested Judith. 'I'll unpack and then get you comfy in bed and bring up a tray of something light. It's been a long day.'

It hadn't occurred to her that there might be difficulties in making Teresa understand about a light supper on a tray. Even with her phrase book and a lot of arm waving and exploring of cupboards, Judith found herself getting nowhere very fast. Teresa was more than willing, but the phrase book wasn't very helpful and there were long delays which she spent thumbing through the pages. Finally Judith went in search of the Professor.

She found him stretched out in a large leather chair drawn up by the open doors in the sitting-room. He looked cool and elegant, and she gave him a cross look. She was untidy and warm and vaguely irritable, a feeling strongly increased by the way in which he got to his feet and looked her up and down with faint smile.

'Poor Judith, you look a little . . .' He left the sentence unfinished in mid-air and she ground her splendid teeth. 'In trouble?' he wanted to know.

'Your mother would like her supper in bed and I think it would be an excellent idea, only I can't find anything in the phrase book that says so—scrambled eggs, too, and creamed potatoes . . .' She had answered him haughtily to begin with, but the haughtiness had petered out with the potatoes. She put up a hand and pushed back her golden hair from a flushed forehead. Suddenly she longed to sit down with a long cool drink while someone else coped. Charles must have read her thoughts.

'Sit down.' He poured something cold and iced from a glass jug on a side table and put it down on the table beside her chair. 'Tell me what you want Teresa to do and I'll tell her. Augusto understands English and speaks a little; he's not here at present, but you'll find that he'll be most helpful.'

'Scrambled egg on thin toast,' said Judith, 'and a little creamed potato and perhaps a tomato salad—no bread, but could she manage a caramel custard or something similar? And wine—I thought a glass of white wine might be nice . . .'

'Vinho Verde—the owner told me that there was some in the cellar.' The Professor sauntered to the door. 'I'll be back presently.'

The drink was delicious, the early evening air cool and scented from the garden. Judith curled up on her chair and closed her eyes.

She woke with an instant feeling of guilt and leapt to her feet, then felt foolish because there was no one there anyway, at least not at that precise moment. Charles Cresswell came through the open door a moment later and remarked in his usual withering tones: 'How guilty you look. I wonder why?'

She ignored this. 'Thank you for organising Lady Cresswell's supper. I'll go and see when she would like it.'

He said nothing, only smiled a little and looked at the ornate clock on the wall behind her. Naturally she looked too, and drew a sharp breath when she saw the time. More than half an hour had elapsed since she had sat down and closed her eyes—but only for a few minutes, surely. Charles had only just returned—the clock was wrong.

'No, it's not,' he told her disconcertingly. 'You've been to sleep; I hadn't the heart to wake you and there was no need, my mother is asleep and you must be tired.' He studied her for a long moment. 'Why not tidy yourself and come down for a drink?'

She was surprised and showed it. 'Well—thank you, but what about Lady Cresswell—if she should wake . . .'

He raised his eyebrows. 'Surely you can deal with that?' he wanted to know. 'Stop fussing and do as I say.'

Rather to her surprise, Judith went meekly upstairs, showered, changed into a cotton crêpe top and wide skirt, arranged her hair with more than usual attention, slapped make-up on to her pretty face, and went downstairs again. Lady Cresswell was still sleeping and she had no idea at what time they were to dine. She found Charles Cresswell bending over a large street plan and he paused only long enough to give her a drink before asking her to look at it. 'Silves is small,' he told her, 'but you will need to find your way around. I have marked the addresses of the people you are most likely to contact. You will find the doctor most helpful and his English is very good. I should contact him about any problem which may arise—and by that I mean not only my mother.'

'Very well. She mentioned several places she wanted to visit again. They're not too far away?'

He shook his head. 'An hour or so in the car at the most. Don't let her travel during the heat of the day, though. The shops close between noon and three o'clock, so encourage her to do her shopping in the evening.' He folded the street plan and gave it to her. 'You're not afraid of the responsibility?'

'No, and I'll take great care of your mother, Professor Cresswell.'

'I know that, Judith, I should never have allowed her to come here otherwise. I trust you completely.'

But he didn't like her. She felt desolate at the thought. 'I'll go to the kitchen and see how Lady Cresswell's supper is getting on,' she told him, and was at the door, to find him beside her.

'If I were to come too,' he murmured, 'it would be easier.'

He was surprisingly helpful; his Portuguese, he told her, was sketchy, all the same he and Teresa seemed to get on very well, and next time, Judith decided, a breakfast or supper tray in bed would present no hazards. She went away presently to find Lady Cresswell awake and wanting her supper and in the best of tempers.

Judith left her eating with an appetite and went downstairs again. She was hungry herself, but the prospect of a meal with the Professor had taken the edge off her appetite. They would make stilted conversation and he would look down his nose at her and snub her with his cold politeness. But she didn't allow her reluctance to show. She walked into the dining room looking cool and serene and very, very pretty, and took her seat opposite him at the round table laid with crisp white linen, shining silver and elegant glasses. The dining room was a good deal smaller than the sitting room, furnished rather sparsely but with great good taste, and the evening sun shone through the wide doors leading to the patio. It shone on Judith's golden hair, and her companion stared at her for a long moment when she turned to look out into the garden. She was, in fact, not looking at the garden at all but feverishly searching for something to say—a wasted exercise, for the Professor leaned back in his chair and embarked on a gentle monologue calculated to put her at ease within minutes. She ate the small dish of salad put before them by Teresa, the swordfish with its delicious sauce, the chicken cooked in cream and wine and the almond and honey tart, in a kind of dream, unable to believe that her charming companion was really Charles Cresswell, and even two glasses of Vinho Verde didn't help, indeed she found herself regarding him with a positively friendly eye and over

coffee, accompanied by something called
Brandymel which he gravely assured her
was a drink composed of honey and brandy,
she allowed her tongue to run away with
her.

'You're being very nice,' she told him.
'Usually you ignore me or snub me.'

He smiled a little. 'I must be feeling well
disposed to everyone this evening.'

Which wasn't the answer she had wanted
to hear.

And it was a little disappointing, after all
that charm, to hear him acquiesce quite
cheerfully to her suggestion that she should
see to her patient and then go to bed herself.
She would keep well out of his way, she
decided. There would be plenty to occupy
her on the following morning and she would
go down early and get breakfast for herself
before anyone was up.

But Teresa was already in the kitchen
when she crept down at seven o'clock and
gave her coffee and rolls as light as air,
sitting on the patio in the glorious morning
sun. And when Teresa came out with the

coffee pot Judith ventured: 'Professor Cresswell?' and received a vague wave of the hand towards the mountains in the distance.

Good, he was out of the house, perhaps for hours. She finished her breakfast at leisure, dressed and went to wake Lady Cresswell.

It was mid-morning, and she had helped her patient dress and then escorted her to a cool corner of the patio and was on her way to the kitchen to get a cold drink for her when the Professor came into the hall through the screened door.

There was no 'good morning'. 'There you are,' he declared, for all the world as though she had been hiding from him. 'How long will you be?'

She eyed him coolly. 'Good morning, Professor Cresswell. Doing what?'

'Whatever you are doing. I want to take you into Silves,' and at her look of disbelief, 'Oh, not for pleasure, I assure you; there are people I think that you should meet before I leave!'

Judith smouldered inwardly. 'I'm getting

a drink for your mother. She may want me to stay with her.'

'She is on the patio.' He strode past her and she heard a murmur of voices as she poured iced lemonade into a frosted jug.

She had hoped that Lady Cresswell might object to her leaving her alone, but on the contrary, that lady seemed to be delighted at the idea of her going into the town with her son. 'Such a good opportunity,' she observed, 'because Charles returns home tomorrow and you'll be without young company for a few weeks. Take a hat with you, dear, the sun's hot.'

Thus dismissed, Judith had nothing more to do but fetch her purse and go downstairs. She had no hat; she supposed she would have to buy one.

The Professor was already behind the wheel, a perfect study of impatience held in check at all costs. He opened the door for her, slammed it shut, waited just long enough for her to fasten her seat belt and set off down the drive. They were half way along the dirt track before he spoke.

'You'll need a hat.'

'So your mother tells me. I hope there'll be time for me to buy one this morning.'

'As long as you don't take all day over it. I think a plain sensible straw is what you need.'

She couldn't stop her chuckle. She said sedately: 'I expect I can choose a hat for myself.'

They went first to the bank where they were received by the manager, given little cups of black coffee and assured that Miss Golightly could depend upon help for anything she might need during their stay. The manager was friendly and impressed by Judith's good looks; he shook hands warmly when they left and begged her to remember that he was her friend. She thanked him prettily, rather more so than she needed to because Charles Cresswell looked so disapproving.

The visit to the doctor was just as successful. He was a youngish man, dark and rather thick set, and made no bones about his admiration for Judith. Since the professor's handsome features still wore a look of remote politeness, she did nothing to discourage him. They arranged a visit to Lady Cresswell for the following day, discussed her illness and her treatment, drank more coffee and took their departure.

The car had been parked on the cobbled stretch below the castle, and since the doctor's house was on the other side of the little town's main road, they had to walk back through narrow streets crowded with people, children, mule carts and dogs. They were waiting at a crossroads when the Professor observed: 'You make friends easily, Judith.' He said it so silkily that she looked at him and encountered a mocking smile.

'Me?' She chose to ignore the mockery. 'Not specially—I like people.' She added: 'You find that hard to believe, I'm sure, you like books.' And before he could reply: 'You're very clever, aren't you? Uncle Tom told me. I expect you find ordinary folk a bore as well as nuisance.' She went on recklessly: 'I'm both, aren't I?'

He didn't answer but shepherded her across the road and once on the other side, said: 'You wished to buy a hat. There's a shop close to the castle which caters for tourists, you'll find one there.'

Judith walked beside him in silence. Her own fault that she had been snubbed, of course. She should have learnt better by now. She told herself that she didn't mind as they went up to the shop through the cobbled street.

It was cool inside and full of the kind of things people want to buy when they are on holiday. Judith prowled round for a minute or two before discovering a table loaded with hats: white cotton ones, like a very small boy's, highly coloured ones, heavily embroidered, plain straw ones ... Mindful of the Professor's preference, she chose a natural straw with a wide brim, paid its modest price and went out into the bright sunshine.

He looked faintly astonished when he saw her. 'You were very quick ...'

'Well, you probably want to get back to

the villa. Besides, it was easy to choose—a plain sensible straw, you said.'

He looked at her, the hat was very becoming. 'It suits you,' he said reluctantly, and then: 'Since we have some time in hand, you might like to look round the cathedral and the castle; neither takes long.'

She followed him into the dim vastness. The cathedral had been built in the Spanish style with a whitewashed exterior and inside it was empty of chairs or pews. Great columns supported its ceiling and there was a small chapel to one side where Henry the Navigator had been buried. Judith liked its bareness, wandering round, quite forgetful of her companion. She remembered him presently and saw him waiting by the door and hurried over, feeling guilty, but all he said was: 'You like it, so do I—it's simple, isn't it?' He led the way out, dropping some coins in the dish an old woman was holding by the door. 'And now the castle.'

It was a stone's throw away; a path between low-growing shrubs and the orange trees Judith still hadn't got used to led them past a crumbling wall and into the ruins of the castle. There wasn't a great deal to see, although she supposed that to a learned scholar like Charles Cresswell, it was of the greatest interest. She asked him one or two questions, but his answers were brief and uttered in an impatient voice so that she gave up after the first few attempts, admired the view and made for the ruined archway which would lead them back to the path. She was ahead of him with the wall on one side of her when she stopped. The wall was full of cracks and niches and in one of these, rather bigger than most, there was a small thin cat with two tiny kittens. The cat mewed at her, looking at her with a resigned hopelessness which brought her to an abrupt halt.

'Has this cat got a home?' she asked the Professor.

'Most unlikely. Cats and dogs aren't ill-treated here, neither are they regarded as household pets.' He looked thoughtfully at the animal. 'She's starving, poor thing—she can hardly hold up her head. Probably she hasn't been able to leave the kittens while she looks for food; they can't be more than a few days old.'

Judith put out a finger and the little cat licked it tiredly. Its mew was plaintive. 'What are we going to do?' she asked him fiercely.

He stood looking down at her, half smiling. 'If you'll take off that highly becoming hat, we could put all three of them into it. I'm sure Teresa won't object to them providing you keep them out of her kitchen.'

No sooner said than done. Judith didn't waste time in thanks, that could come later. Mother and kittens needed urgent attention if they were to survive. She carried them carefully, too weak to protest, to where the car had been parked, and got in carefully, her hat on her knees. Half way to the villa she asked: 'Do you think we'll get her well again? She isn't too starved?'

'You'll get her well, Judith, I have no doubt of that. I shan't be here.'

'Oh—you're leaving tomorrow?'

'This evening.'

She was astonished to find that she didn't want him to go, but it would be just as well—he was growing on her; impatience, ill humour, mockery, the lot. She said 'Oh,' again and then: 'Thank you very much for letting me have this little cat and her kittens. I'm very grateful. Do you think I'm very silly? You don't approve of sentimental people, do you?'

'I'm not above modifying my opinions,' he told her, 'I dislike mawkishness. And I don't consider you silly, Judith. I would have done exactly the same.'

She turned to look at him. 'You would?' Her astonishment made him wince.

Lady Cresswell, told about the tiny creatures still in Judith's hat, was instantly diverted. Teresa was sent for, a box was requested, a saucer of powdered milk, suitably warmed, was fetched, and the cat and her kittens gently transferred to their new quarters and the mother fed. She supped languidly, but she purred too. Judith said anxiously: 'Do you suppose we've got her in time? She's all skin and bone.'

'With regular light meals and plenty of water she stands a very good chance.' Charles Cresswell, standing with his hands in his pockets, moved towards the door. 'I'll go and talk to Teresa and suggest that you make yourself responsible for this creature's food and well being.'

When he had gone Judith asked: 'You don't mind, Lady Cresswell? We couldn't leave her . . .'

'Of course I don't mind, child—Charles has been bringing home lost and sick animals since he was a very small boy. His dogs were both abandoned—both past their first youth when he found them too.'

Judith paused in the pouring of a cool drink for Lady Cresswell. 'I've just thought—what will happen when we go back . . .?'

She hadn't seen the Professor standing in the open door leading to the patio. 'They'll have to go into quarantine, of course,' he observed 'and then presently take up residence at Hawkshead.'

Judith beamed at him. 'Oh, they'll love it there—how kind you are!'

His smile mocked her. 'You overwhelm me, Judith.'

She bent her head over the box, feeling the colour flooding her face. Presently she put the box down, murmured about fetching more milk and went away without looking at him.

When she went back, almost half an hour later, he had gone. She fed the cat again, read the most interesting bits from the English papers they had brought back with them and then sat idly chatting until Lady Cresswell dozed off. There was another feed due by then. Judith went to the kitchen once more, this time for chicken broth, fed her charge, pleased to see that she was looking more lively already, and then went to get writing paper and pen. She had started on a letter home when the Professor returned.

'If that's to your parents, let me have it and I'll post it in England. But why not ring them up? The telephone's in the hall and there's another in the small room behind the dining room they call the study.' He smiled at her, this time with no mockery. 'Off you go now—I want to talk to mother when she wakes up anyway.'

Judith allowed herself to be dismissed and went along to the study where she had a long and satisfying chat with her mother and then, since no one had asked for her, went through a side door into the garden, where she lay on the beautifully tended grass and let the sun drench her. She should have used her Ambre Solaire and worn a hat, but she didn't think it mattered. A view not shared by Charles Cresswell, who came strolling towards her a little later. 'You'll have a headache and look like a lobster if you don't move into the shade,' he told her forthrightly. 'I'll allow that you're not a conceited girl, but who wants to look a figure of fun? Besides, it's painful.'

She scrambled to her feet, feeling a fool. 'I never do anything right, do I?' she demanded snappishly, and stalked off indoors, to rush to her room and inspect her face and person for signs of sunburn.

They lunched, the three of them, in the shade of the patio, on a cold fish salad and a light-as-air pudding called Mountain Rose.

Charles Cresswell waved a hand in the direction of the mountains in the distance. 'The Monchiques are covered with them—rather like our own wild rose, but butter-coloured—hence the pudding's name.' He had talked more than usual, perhaps because his mother, although she said very little about it, didn't want him to go. He had teased her into a cheerful frame of mind by the time the meal was over, and Judith, escorting her to her darkened, air-conditioned room for a nap, was pleased to see that. She offered pills and a cool drink, assured Lady Cresswell that she would rouse her in good time for tea, and went along to her own room. She had no particular wish to stay there, but she was reasonably sure that the Professor wouldn't want her company. She had brought the cat and the kittens upstairs before lunch, together with a supply of nourishing food. Now she attended to the little creature's wants, watched it settle down once more with a protecting paw over the kittens, and went out on to the balcony.

It was very hot. She supposed she would have to stay in her room unless Charles went out. She leaned over and carefully inspected the garden and as much of the patio below as she could see. She was about to withdraw her head when he stepped from directly under her balcony and looked up at her.

'Yes, I'm still here. Afraid to come down, Judith?'

She replied with something of a snap, 'Certainly not! I was just looking around . . .'

'In that case get your bathing things and come and have a swim in the pool.'

She hesitated for a couple of seconds, but the prospect was too inviting. She nodded and went to find her bikini.

The pool was large, the water warm and she swam well. Beyond a brief greeting, the

Professor had had nothing to say, but had plunged in from the side and was swimming strongly away from her. Judith pulled on her cap and dived in from the board at one end, passing him halfway going in the opposite direction. They did this several times and she began to wonder if he thought he was alone; he could at least pass the time of day ... She hoisted herself out by the board and went and stood on it.

Her bikini was a brilliant blue, beautifully cut and did her figure full justice, but as far as he was concerned, she suspected that an old sack would have done just as well. As he swam towards her, she sprang up and down on the board without actually diving in; she had very little vanity, but just for once she would have liked him to have made some comment—that she could swim well, that he liked the colour of her bikini, that he could see her, even ...

'Why are you leaping up and down like a scalded cat?' he wanted to know, and before she could answer that, had turned and begun his powerful journey back to the other end.

He hadn't quite reached it when she nipped off the board, picked up her towel and went back to the house. He was rude, intolerant, pigheaded, and thank heaven he was going back to England within a few hours! She was glad, thrilled to bits, she wouldn't have to put up with his company for three weeks. She stopped dead in her tracks, suddenly aware that three weeks was a lifetime, longer than that. He would be miles away and she wouldn't see him or know what he was doing or who he was with. That beastly Eileen Hunt, probably. When she saw him again, if she ever did, he might be going to marry the girl; at best, he would have forgotten her. Judith stood on the stairs, wrapped in her towel, dripping gently. Charles wasn't going until the evening, he had said, so she would see him again, perhaps she would have a chance to tell him... Tell him what? she thought wildly. That she had just discovered that she was head over heels in love with him?

Tiresome, ill-tempered creature that he was. And she could imagine that mocking smile and the blandly spoken answer she'd get to that!

She went on up the stairs to her room, had a shower and dressed, and outwardly looking cool and self-possessed, went down to the patio. Await events, her father had always advised her when she had been uncertain of something, and that was exactly what she intended doing.

It was very quiet. Teresa and Augusto were having their midday rest, the cat and kittens were peacefully sleeping, so was Lady Cresswell—she had peeped in to see. And of Charles Cresswell there was no sign. At four o'clock she went to wake Lady Cresswell, fed the cat and went to the kitchen to ask for the tea tray to be brought to the patio, and over the tea things she learned that Charles had gone to Silves on some business of his own. 'He'll be back shortly,' observed Lady Cresswell. 'He told me he wants to have a little talk before he goes.'

Which was her nice way of warning Judith to keep out of the way. Judith was at the other end of the garden, cutting roses in the early evening cool, when she heard the car start up. She didn't give it a second thought. Charles wouldn't go without saying goodbye, even if they weren't on the best of terms. She cut a few more roses, rehearsing the little speech she was going to make to him; she had thought it out carefully and she hoped that hearing it, he would understand that she would like to be friends in future. Once they were friends, who knew what might happen?

She wandered back to the house and found Lady Cresswell in the sitting room, reading a novel. 'There you are, dear,' she remarked a little too brightly. 'Shall we get out the backgammon board? I always feel a little low when Charles goes.'

'Goes?' asked Judith woodenly.

'Why, yes, dear—about ten minutes ago.' She peeped at Judith's downcast face and allowed herself the faintest of pleased smiles. 'We shall miss him.'

CHAPTER SEVEN

JUDITH had never been much good at backgammon, and that evening she was quite hopeless. Lady Cresswell won with no trouble at all, elected to stay downstairs for dinner and then sat for a little while with the tiny cat and her kittens in their box beside her. Judith guessed that she was missing her son more than she would admit and probably faced a bad night. But she went to bed finally after an hour of making plans for the next week or two, and Judith stayed with her for a while, pottering softly around the room, carrying on a murmured conversation until Lady Cresswell finally went to sleep. She went to her own room then, settling her charges on the balcony with the door open. It was a warm night and they would come to no harm. She gave the cat a final small meal, stroked the scraggy little head and went to bed herself, to lie awake and think of Charles. He would be back in England by now. She wondered where he would spend the night and wished she knew more about him; his life was something of which she knew very little. An historian of some repute, living a comfortable life with sufficient money to do as he pleased, possessed of a number of friends—beyond that she could only guess. A useless exercise anyway.

Presently she got out of her bed and went to sit on the balcony. There was a moon, almost full, and the garden, dim in its light, smelled delicious. She could make out the mountains not so very far away and lower down the faint lights of Silves. It was quiet too, so that the occasional rustle from the cats' box sounded loud. Judith stayed for some time, trying to sort out her thoughts and getting nowhere. She made no bones about being in love with Charles; she was, and that was an end to it. It was a silly thing to do and she couldn't think why she had done it. He had given her no encouragement at all, and he would make a by no means perfect husband. The thing was to do something sensible about it, like forgetting him. She contemplated this idea briefly and threw it out. Charles wasn't a man one could forget easily, whatever one's feelings towards him were. Getting as far away as possible from him was more sensible, only she couldn't do that just yet. Lady Cresswell had to be considered. Judith had grown fond of the valiant little lady and had no intention of giving her even the smallest worry for the limited time that she had left to her. That might mean months and she wasn't sure what was worse—the prospect of trying to avoid Charles whenever possible, or seeing him every day and pretending that she had no interest in him whatever. She decided that they were as bad as each other, which made the future look gloomy. She had three weeks, of course, before they returned to England, and perhaps Lady Cresswell would decide to stay in her own home in London, which would solve the problem nicely. She doubted if they would spend the winter in Cumbria and perhaps if she didn't see him for weeks on end he would fade... Upon due reflection she came to the conclusion that the Professor wasn't a man to fade. She sighed and went back to bed. She had always prided herself on her good sense, but that didn't stop her having a good cry.

But there was no sign of her sleepless night the next morning. She swam in the pool, drank her morning tea, saw to the cats' wants, dressed and went to see how Lady Cresswell was. Surprisingly cheerful, as it turned out, full of plans for a drive up into the mountains within the next few days, a visit to the spa, a drive down to the coast, and perhaps a picnic there. 'You could have a swim,' she encouraged Judith. 'We'll go to Praia da Rocha, there's a lovely beach there, and perhaps it would be better if we had lunch at the Algarve Hotel. We'll do that tomorrow. Charles said I wasn't to do anything today, so I won't.'

'The doctor's coming to see you,' Judith

reminded her. 'He said he'd be here some time after three o'clock.'

Lady Cresswell nodded. 'He can have tea with us. I'm going to lie in the shade this morning and do nothing.' She sat up. 'No, better still, you shall splash around in the pool and I'll watch you.'

So the morning passed pleasantly enough. Judith swam and dived and lolled around with a watchful eye on her companion and her thoughts miles away. Charles would be on his way home by now, already there, perhaps. They were having lunch on the patio when he telephoned. Judith, who had answered the phone, felt the colour rush to her face when she heard his cool voice. 'Judith, I should like to speak to my mother.'

No 'Hullo', or 'How are you?' She said in a voice equally impersonal: 'I'll fetch her,' and did so, making her comfortable in a chair before going out of the room. There was a great lump in her chest like heavy dough. She wanted to run out of the house, go back to England, to her home, to the hospital, to the time before she had met him. When she heard Lady Cresswell calling to her she went back, half hoping that he wanted to speak to her too, but Lady Cresswell had hung up.

Dr Sebastiao arrived punctually, and because Judith was lonely and unhappy she responded to his quite obvious admiration. He examined his patient with great care and thoroughness, took a sample of blood, stayed to tea, entertaining them with lighthearted talk about Portugal and Algarve in particular, and suggested that they might like to go for a drive one evening, then took himself off.

'He took a fancy to you, Judith,' commented Lady Cresswell as they watched him race away down the drive. 'He's a very nice man; I hope he invites you out for an evening.'

Judith smiled and nodded vaguely. Why was it, she wondered, that a man you had not the least interest in chatted you up whenever you met, and someone you desperately wanted to like you—even notice

you—behaved as though you were yesterday's cold potatoes?

'How old did you say you were, dear?'
asked Lady Cresswell suddenly.

Judith looked at her in considerable
astonishment. 'Twenty-seven—halfway to
twenty-eight, actually.'

She was still more astonished at Lady
Cresswell's satisfied: 'Just the right age.'

Judith was dying to ask the obvious
question, but on occasion her patient could
be as withdrawn as her son. She decided to
say nothing, and spent the remainder of the
day consumed with curiosity.

They went to Praia da Rocha the
following morning, driven by Augusto in
the car hired by Charles before he left. It
wasn't too hot as yet and the country was a
feast of colour and the grape harvest was in
full swing, almonds were being gathered,
and figs, and there were flowers everywhere.
Even the smallest cottage had its garden
with a vine trailing over the porch, orange
and lemon trees casting a welcome shade in
which a mixture of vegetables and flowers

grew. 'Isn't it funny,' observed Judith, 'that with so much colour around them, the women all wear black?' She gazed at a group of women standing by the road. 'And their black felt hats!'

'To keep off the sun,' explained Lady Cresswell. 'And I expect most of them are widows.' She added: 'Charles would be able to answer all your questions. Such a pity that he isn't here.'

And Judith silently agreed.

They drove through Portimao before they reached the sea—a bustling little town, famous for its sardine fisheries. The harbour was full of fishing boats hung with nets, each with its eye painted on the prow. Judith would have liked to explore the town, but probably she would have the chance before they went back. They were near the sea by now, the white villas with their red-tiled roofs were scattered thickly and there were several tower blocks to which Lady Cresswell took instant exception. But they were forgotten as they rounded the ancient fort facing out to sea below the harbour and they saw the great sweep of golden sand and the blue sea beyond. There weren't a great many people about, the height of the season had passed and the children were back at school. 'You're going to enjoy this,' declared Lady Cresswell. 'We'll go to the hotel and have coffee and order lunch and I shall sit on the terrace while you swim. You can go from the hotel, of course.'

It would never have entered Judith's head to use the hotel, but when they went in its rather grand entrance, nothing could have been easier. Lady Cresswell was escorted on to a shady terrace overlooking the beach and the pair of them had coffee before Judith went away to change for her swim.

The sea was warm and as smooth as silk; she swam until she was tired and then padded back to the terrace.

'That's a very eye-catching bikini,' remarked Lady Cresswell. 'You've a splendid shape, my dear. I daresay the sea is a great deal nicer than the pool at the villa.'

Judith was lying on a sunbed letting the

sun sink into the seawater and Ambre
Solaire. 'Much nicer,' she agreed.

'But I daresay you enjoyed your swim
with Charles?' persisted Lady Cresswell.
She had a high clear voice and sometimes
there was a note in it which compelled an
answer.

'We quarrelled,' said Judith briefly.

'Dear, dear,' murmured her companion.
'Of course, dear Charles can be most vexing
at times.' She took off her sunglasses and
polished them carefully. 'All the same, I
miss him—he seems such a very long way
away.'

Dark glasses were useful things, thought
Judith, one could hide behind them. She
said carefully: 'Only a little under three
hours by plane. I expect he's getting a lot of
work done.' Despite herself, there was a
note of bitterness in her voice.

'I'm not sure of that,' said his mother,
and smiled a little.

Judith hadn't seen the smile. 'I'll go and
change,' she said. 'I won't be a minute. Can
I do anything for you before I go?'

'No, dear. We'll have a cool drink when you get back and decide what we're going to eat. After lunch I'd like to look round the boutique . . .'

'Of course, but a rest first, don't you think?' Judith lingered by her chair. 'Would you like to do anything later on?'

'Augusto will drive us through the town after tea, if we see a shop we like the look of we can always get him to stop. We might see some books.'

Judith eyed her carefully; she was standing up well to the days activities and she didn't look tired. 'Yes, let's do that,' she agreed cheerfully.

They lunched in a cool dining room, off iced melon, a fish salad and ice cream, and had coffee on the terrace again, and presently Lady Cresswell dozed off in her shady corner while Judith lay in the sun. It was very hot, she could feel the heat through her thin sleeveless dress, but she had rubbed in more sun lotion and popped her straw hat on to her head. She had a thick creamy skin which didn't burn easily and she wanted to go home with a splendid tan. Presently she slept.

They had tea later and then, as it grew cooler, they went to inspect the boutique in the foyer. Judith bought a handful of cards to send to friends and family, but Lady Cresswell ignored them. She could telephone, she pointed out, so much easier and quicker than all that writing. More expensive too, but she wasn't concerned with that. She turned over the dainty mats and cloths and bought several, as well as some pottery she liked the look of, and finally she bought half a dozen exquisitely embroidered handkerchiefs and gave them to Judith. It all cost a staggeringly large sum of money, but that only whetted Lady Cresswell's appetite to do a little more shopping. Augusto was instructed to drive slowly along the promenade until a bookshop was found, where they spent a considerable time while she chose a dozen paperbacks. 'And get whatever you want for yourself, dear,' she told Judith, who, feeling very much in the mood for that sort of thing, chose Jilly Cooper's *The British in Love*.

They went home after that because Lady Cresswell looked tired. Judith whisked her off to bed and bore up a supper tray presently. 'A lovely day,' she observed cheerfully, 'but let's have a lazy day tomorrow. I have got dozens of postcards to write, and Teresa has promised me she'll show me how to make Mountain Rose pudding—at least I think that's what she said.'

Lady Cresswell agreed readily enough—perhaps she had done too much, thought Judith worriedly, but her pulse and temperature were normal and there was no sign of purpura. She would see how things were in the morning and if she still felt uneasy she would get Dr Sebastiao to call in the morning.

She ate her own dinner, with one ear listening for her patient's bell and the other for the telephone—just in case Charles rang up. But he didn't, and in the morning Lady Cresswell was quite recovered. All the same, Judith kept to the plan and they spent a quiet day reading and talking and listening to the record player, and at lunchtime Charles did telephone, wasting no time on her at all, merely asking to speak to his mother. Judith sat there, peeling an orange, shutting her ears to Lady Cresswell's voice saying yes and no, willing him to ask for her. But he didn't, and she was forced to listen to her companion's vague account of how busy he was with his book—the research was going well. 'Oh, and he asked after the little cat, Judith—I said she was doing very well and so were the kittens. Shouldn't we find a name for her—for all of them, since they'll be coming to live with us?' She frowned. 'Something English.'

'Mrs Smith,' suggested Judith without giving it much thought, 'that's very English—and call the kittens George and Mary.'

'What a good idea—they're so sweet, even Teresa likes them.' Lady Cresswell sipped her coffee. 'What shall we do tomorrow, Judith?'

'You'd like to go somewhere?'

'Indeed yes. Shall we go to Caldas and drink the water? I believe it's quite fashionable nowadays, although I can't think why. It's off the main road and only a small village.'

'It's not far from here?'

'No distance at all. Shall we go in the morning and have lunch and come home directly after?'

'That sounds fun . . .'

Lady Cresswell interrupted her: 'And we must go to Monchique.'

'On another day, perhaps? Didn't you tell me there's an inn there where we can have tea and look at the view?'

Lady Cresswell agreed enthusiastically. 'And we must go to the sea again so that you can swim, and there are several towns— Sagres and Lagos and Albufeira. I do hope that nice Dr Sebastiao takes you out, Judith.'

'Well, you know, I'm happy just to be here and do nothing all day, being bone idle is such a delightful experience—besides, the pool here is quite super.' Judith got up and gave her arm to her companion. 'I shall have a swim while you're taking your nap.'

It was lonely in the pool. She swam up and down and thought about Charles; sitting with his handsome nose buried in some dry-as-dust old tome, she supposed. On the other hand, he might be dallying with Eileen Hunt—the girl had a clear field and time enough to mug up bits about the thirteenth century so that she could look intelligent when he enthused about churches and Magna Carta and feudal Law . . .

She was suddenly tired of the pool; she got out and lay in the sun drying and then went indoors to dress. Lady Cresswell was still asleep and to stay indoors seemed a great waste of the splendid weather. Judith found her hat and wandered off down the drive and along the dirt track towards the road. She turned away from the direction of Silves and strolled along towards the mountains, meeting no one, and no houses in sight. The dog coming towards her was the only thing moving, and he was doing that in a tired way that made her stand still and look at him. He wore no collar; and Charles had told her that all dogs in Portugal had to wear a collar if they were owned, although some of the owners didn't bother, but this animal looked as if it wasn't owned. He was a large, loosely put together animal, not so very young and sorely in need of a bath and a good brush and, more than these, a good meal. He advanced towards Judith in a hopeful way and after a glance at her face, trotted along beside her. And when she turned for home presently, he turned too.

She was a tender-hearted girl and at times impulsive, so she allowed him to accompany her back to the villa, where, no one being about, she filled an old plate with odds and ends of food and took it out to where he was waiting patiently at the back door. He paused just long enough to wag his thin pointed tail before wolfing down the lot and then he looked at her so hopefully that she went back to the kitchen and piled the plate again. He ate that too and then sat down watching her; it was obvious that he considered himself her dog. She led him to a corner of the garden where he wouldn't be seen immediately, for Teresa would be coming presently to get their tea and Judith wasn't sure if he would be welcome. 'Be a good quiet boy,' she begged him, and hurried upstairs.

Lady Cresswell was awake and in splendid spirits and it took less than a minute to explain about the dog and ask, a little warily, if there was any chance of keeping him. 'He would be nice to have about the house—and he's gentle enough, only scruffy and tired.'

'Why not?' Agreed Lady Cresswell. 'He'll be company for Mrs Smith and the kittens—it's a splendid idea. Send Teresa to me, dear, and I'll do my best to explain.'

'Oh, thank you, Lady Cresswell—if we could just feed him up a bit . . .'

'He can come back with us,' declared Lady Cresswell. 'Charles won't mind.'

'But how could we get them back?'

'We can always charter a plane, dear.'

The dog was still there, he didn't appear

to have moved an inch. Anxious to make the most of his looks, Judith found a brush and did her best with his appearance. His coat was dull and dusty, but at least she smoothed it to some sort of order and he submitted quietly enough. He cringed a little when Lady Cresswell joined them, but upon Judith begging him not to be a silly boy he wagged a tail and flung out his boney chest so that Teresa, who had followed Lady Cresswell, had to admit that there seemed no harm in him. He wasn't a local dog, of that she was sure; most likely turned loose at some time or other, but provided he behaved himself and didn't go into her kitchen, she gave her grudging approval to his joining the household.

So Judith went in search of Augusto to find a lead and a collar and a place for the dog to sleep and, since he still looked hungry, another plate of food. He went and sat quietly by Lady Cresswell after that, and even the arrival of Mrs Smith and her kittens, carried out in their box to take the cooler air after tea, left him unmoved. It kept Lady Cresswell nicely occupied and interested until dinner time, and when Charles telephoned soon after that meal, Judith heard her telling him about the dog, even out on the patio Lady Cresswell's high clear voice carried.

They were to keep the animal, Lady Cresswell told her triumphantly, and he was to return with them when they went home. 'I told dear Charles that chartering a plane to take us all back was a small price to pay for the pleasure I get from the creatures.' She twinkled at Judith. 'I think if I asked for the moon, Charles would climb into the sky and get it for me. He has his faults, but he is a good son and he'll be a good husband.'

'Oh, is he thinking of getting married?' Judith hoped her voice sounded unconcerned.

'Oh, definitely, my dear.' Lady Cresswell peeped at her quickly. 'At least, when I say he's thinking about it, he doesn't know that he is, if you understand me. These clever men are sometimes so slow to see something any ordinary person would have discovered in no time at all. And now I think I'll go to bed; we'll make an early start in the morning, shall we? And perhaps we'd better take the dog with us—the quicker he knows he belongs to us the better. You won't mind taking him on a lead?' She added: 'Charles does hope he's house-trained!'

Something Judith hadn't thought of; he was hardly a dog to grace a home such as Charles's either. Perhaps it would be a good idea if she took him over once they were in England, and there was the question of the cat and kittens too. He had said that they might find a home with him, but if he was going to marry and if his bride was to be the horrible Eileen, the chances were that an outcast dog and a tatty moggy would be shown the door. Not by Charles, of course—she gave him that—he wouldn't be intentionally unkind, but if he was besotted he might not even notice. She put the problem aside and allowed his austere image to fill her mind—something done with such success that she didn't fall asleep until the small hours.

They left for Caldas very shortly after breakfast, for Lady Cresswell professed herself full of energy and anxious to start. Judith spent a busy hour, getting that lady ready for her day's outing, attending to Mrs Smith and the kittens, feeding the dog, brushing him and installing him, to his great surprise, in the car. She prudently laid an old blanket on the seat first and he seemed to know what was wanted of him, because he curled up at once. With a collar on and a few good meals inside him he looked more presentable, although it was obvious that the variety of his ancestry was without number. Studying him, Judith asked: 'Do you suppose the Professor will mind having him? He's—well, he's not exactly handsome.'

Lady Cresswell looked over her shoulder at her. 'Charles will take him. He said so; he never goes back on his word.'

Judith hadn't known what to expect at the spa, a miniature Baden-Baden perhaps as

she remembered it on T.V., certainly not
the quaint little village away from the main
road with a cluster of white-walled and
stone buildings and a small modern hospital
beyond. Augusto parked the car on the
cobbled road and they walked the few yards
to a square surrounded by buildings and
with two lines of trees shading a row of seats
down its centre, presumably for the comfort
of those desirous of drinking the water.
There was a restaurant, a café and two
shops, already doing a brisk trade with
visitors. But Lady Cresswell ignored these.
'The water first,' she observed, and took a
path away from the square to a small glass-
roofed building.

'Will they let the dog in?' asked Judith.
They both stopped to look at him, not a
prepossessing creature but very docile.

'Why not?' asked Lady Cresswell, used to
getting her own way.

In fact no one noticed him. There
were few people there; they walked in,
obediently took their glasses, sipped the
sulphur-flavoured water under the eye of

the lady behind the counter and went out again.

'A cool drink?' suggested Lady Cresswell. 'I'd forgotten how nauseating spa waters can be. These, by the way, are supposed to make you ten years younger.'

Judith laughed. 'Well, so they should, they taste beastly enough!'

They had their drinks sitting in the little square at one of the tables outside the café. It was pleasantly cool and the dog had subsided thankfully at their feet and was sleeping. Lounging on a wall some distance from them a young man, long-haired and burnt brown by the sun, was playing *Greensleeves*, on a tin whistle. He played well and the charming little tune tore at Judith's unhappy heart. Not wanting to hear any more of it she asked: 'Shall I get you another drink? It's so pleasant sitting here . . .'

Lady Cresswell didn't want anything else, she wanted to browse round the two shops. 'Not that I want anything,' she remarked vaguely, 'but we might as well have a look while we're here.'

So they strolled across the square and the young man waved them goodbye and Judith waved back. She tied the dog to a tree before they went inside, and Lady Cresswell said: 'We must give him a name—something suitable . . .'

'Something typically English, so that he'll feel he's one of us,' suggested Judith. 'How about George or Arthur?'

Lady Cresswell considered. 'Arthur—it suits him.' She patted his head. 'Good boy, Arthur.'

The shop was really only a room in a cottage, but it was full of enticing things to buy. Lady Cresswell spent a long time wandering from embroidered teacloths to pottery, from carved wooden boxes to knitted jackets and shawls, before she decided to buy something of everything. Judith, leaving Arthur to keep Lady Cresswell company, took their parcels back to the car and had to rouse a somnolent Augusto to open the door.

It was getting warmer now and she suggested that they might sit in the shade for half an hour before they had lunch—a light meal of salad, fish and ices. By now Lady Cresswell was tiring and it didn't take much to persuade her to get into the car and be driven back to the villa, where Judith lost no time in making her comfortable on her bed for an afternoon nap. And, that done, she saw to the animals, got into her swimsuit and spent half an hour in the pool before going to lie on the patio. It would have to be a quiet day tomorrow, she decided, and probably the next one as well.

It seemed as though Lady Cresswell was content to idle her days away now that she had had an outing or two, and as the following day was more than usually warm, she was content to sit in a shady corner of the garden, reading and gossiping and amusing herself with the animals, and on the day after that, although she expressed a wish to drive up into the mountains, Judith was able to dissuade her without much trouble. They ate out of doors and played backgammon and talked about clothes, and Judith was relieved to see that her companion was her usual bright self again. There would be days like that, she knew, when Lady Cresswell would be tired and a trifle irritable, and as time went on they would become more frequent, but they could be faced and dealt with; meanwhile, Lady Cresswell was holding her own nicely. 'It's so nice to have you, Judith,' she observed. 'I can talk to you, I don't have to pretend and you always know when I'm frightened, don't you? Not often now, though. I feel so well for most of the time, it's hard to believe . . .'

'You're holding your own,' Judith told her, 'and that's more important than anything else. Talk about it if you want to; I'll help you all I can, you know that.'

They smiled at each other in mutual understanding.

They played an hilarious game of Racing Demon that second evening and Lady Cresswell went to bed later than usual. Judith came downstairs again into the quiet house. For Augusto and Teresa had gone to bed and only Mrs Smith and her kittens, snug in the kitchen, were waiting for a last drink of milk, and Arthur, sitting watchfully in the hall, waited too, knowing that a last snack before bed would be offered him. Judith saw to Mrs Smith, fetched a handful of biscuits from the kitchen and went into the sitting room with Arthur. It was a lovely night, warm and bright, with a full moon, and she opened the doors on to the patio at the back of the house. It was quiet too, if one ignored the crickets. She leaned her elbows on the patio railing and looked at the moon, and Arthur came crowding up to her to thrust his rough head against her. He had been bathed for the second time and at last he was beginning to look less like a scarecrow. He growled now, low in his throat, and at the same time Judith heard a car coming up the dirt track. She caught its headlights in the glass doors as a reflection, as she went indoors and shut them and crossed the hall. It might be the doctor, but she didn't think so—not at almost eleven o'clock at night. It might be Charles Cresswell—he hadn't phoned for a couple of days, but she thought that unlikely. She waited for the door bell to ring, but although she had distinctly heard the car stop there was no sound. She stood in the hall, staring at the door, just a little scared and glad to have Arthur's company. He growled again and she turned at the faint sound behind her. Charles Cresswell was standing in the sitting room doorway, watching her.

She said in a tight voice, 'Why didn't you ring the bell instead of creeping in like a thief—scaring me to death?'

He put his hands in his pockets. 'I credited you with more sense. Who else would come as late as this, anyway? And thieves don't usually drive up in a car and park outside the front door. I saw the light in the sitting room and thought you were there.' His eyes moved from her face to Arthur. 'Good God, what have you got there?'

'Arthur—the dog your mother told you about. He's a very good dog—he growled. I daresay if I told him to he'd bite you.'

The Professor laughed softly. 'You look as though you'd like to do that yourself. Always so welcoming, Judith.' He took a hand from his pocket and snapped his fingers, and Arthur went to him at once and stood gazing up at him as though he worshipped him. 'At least the dog likes me,' observed the Professor. 'Aren't you going to ask me why I'm here?'

'No, it's none of my business. Do you want a drink or something to eat?'

'The perfect hostess! No, thank you, I'll get myself a drink and go to bed. Is my mother in good spirits?'

'Yes. Dr Sebastiao is quite satisfied with her, she's been resting for the last two days, but only because it's been warmer than usual.'

He nodded. 'Then we'll say goodnight, shall we? Where does Arthur sleep?'

'In the kitchen with the cats.'

'I'll see to him.' He moved from the doorway and came towards her. 'Thank you, Judith, for taking such good care of my mother. I appreciate it.'

He bent his head and kissed her surprised mouth, presumably to show his appreciation. It left her shaken and trembling so that she hurried away and up the stairs without looking at him.

CHAPTER EIGHT

NATURALLY enough, Judith spent a rather sleepless night and got up early. The house was quiet and there was no one about as she went down to the kitchen and put on the kettle for a cup of tea. The animals woke at once, of course, and sat looking at her with hopeful eyes until she produced their food and opened the door to let Mrs Smith and Arthur out into the garden. They were back before she had made the tea, still not quite believing that the door wasn't going to be shut in their faces. She told them briskly that they were a silly pair, gave them second helpings and bore her tea tray upstairs, to have it taken from her when she reached the landing by the Professor, wearing a dressing gown of subdued magnificence.

'Be a good girl and fetch another cup,' he said. 'I'll take this in to my mother.'

'Good morning,' said Judith pointedly. 'Your mother is probably still asleep.'

'Then I'll wake her up.' He stood looking at her. 'That's a pretty thing you're wearing. Shall we have a swim in the pool before breakfast?'

She remembered the last time and went pink. 'No—I've got several things to do. I'll get another cup . . .'

And when she went back again with it: 'Why only one? Don't you have tea in the morning?'

She was suddenly irritable. 'Yes, of course I do. That's my tray, I was taking it to my room. Your mother doesn't have hers until eight o'clock.'

'*Mea culpa!*' He didn't look in the least sorry.

'And stop showing off your Latin, because I'm not listening.'

She ran downstairs again, furious because he was laughing gently at her, closed the door and put the kettle on again. He was horrid, the most unpleasant man she had ever met, thoughtless and arrogant and making her feel a fool. She was quite mad to love him, and what a frightful waste of time that was—and probably if he ever found out he'd laugh and make some snubbing remark in a silky voice. She drank her tea, still in a rage, and then crept upstairs to her room, changed into a bikini and went down to the pool. She met him, as she hoped she would, as she was going back into the house, and swept past him with as much dignity as she could muster, draped as she was in a large towel and her hair streaming wetly all over the place. She didn't look at him as she went past, or she might have stopped at the look on his face.

When she went along to Lady Cresswell's room, it was to find that Lady in a state of happy excitement. 'Only imagine, coming late last night! I was so very pleased to see him this morning—and just think, he's going to drive us to Monchique this afternoon. I think I'll get up a little earlier today, dear, I feel so well. If I have my breakfast now I'll be ready to dress by the time you've had yours.'

Judith turned a serene face to hers. 'Pills and chores first,' she said cheerfully, 'then I'll get your breakfast tray. Are you going to sit in the garden in that nice shady corner, or would you perhaps prefer the patio?'

'Oh, the garden, I think, we've such a lot to talk about you can have an hour to yourself, dear.'

'And Arthur can do with a walk. I'll go down the road and follow that track on the other side where the orange groves are.'

The Professor joined her for breakfast, maintaining a polite flow of conversation, all of it trivial. It was the kind of talk two strangers might have exchanged, sharing a hotel table, and she was heartily relieved when he said that he had to go into Silves to see the doctor and left her to drink her last cup of tea alone.

He was back before Lady Cresswell came downstairs, sitting in a cane chair in her usual corner. He got to his feet as she joined him and helped her to arrange herself just so, while Judith disposed of the variety of articles necessary for a morning in the garden, and when she had done that she fetched Mrs Smith and the kittens.

Lady Cresswell examined them narrowly. 'They're looking well, Judith. We're going to have lunch a little later, so don't hurry back. You'll take Arthur with you?'

Judith said she would, said goodbye without looking at the Professor and went to get Arthur's lead. At any other time she would have been delighted to have had a couple of hours to herself, but she couldn't get rid of the suspicion that they were going to discuss her. If Charles was going to marry Eileen Hunt she wouldn't be wanted, she was sure of that. His would be the task of persuading his mother that other plans for her future comfort would be just as satisfactory as having Judith. And to a man in love these would be perfectly feasible; he must think that his Eileen was a paragon among women, willing to devote herself to her mother-in-law. His mother had said that he was too clever to see things that the less bright cottoned on to at once, and she should know. 'He needs someone to look after him,' she observed to Arthur, and was comforted by the understanding look that he gave her.

They had crossed the road and were quite a distance from it, going towards the line of cork trees half way up the foothills, when the sky began to fill with cloud. Judith hurried her steps. There was plenty of shelter ahead of them and if it were to rain she could take cover easily enough.

It began before she was half way there, with Arthur trotting along beside her, just as anxious to get out of the wet as she was. It was no light drizzle either, but a downpour that soaked them both within seconds. What was more, there was a rumble of thunder and then lightning zigzagging across the sky.

Under the trees at last, they made shift to shake themselves dry and then sat down on a patch of ground, trying to keep away from the great drops falling between the branches. 'It won't last,' Judith told Arthur reassuringly, and peered around for a sign of blue sky. There was none; the rain was as drenching as ever and the storm seemed to be almost overhead. It was a fortunate thing that she wasn't particularly nervous of thunder and lightning, because Arthur was. He had got as close as he possibly could to her, and shivered at each flash. But even Judith was scared speechless as a nearby tree was struck by lightning and some of its branches came tumbling down. There was no time to get away. She slung her arms about Arthur's hairy chest and ducked her head.

Most of the branches fell clear of them, but by some freak of fate, the last to fall, a solid forked branch, fell squarely across Judith's ankles, not harming them but imprisoning them just as surely as iron fetters. She had let out a frightened shout, but now she sat up and leaned forward as far as she could to free herself. But it was no good, she couldn't get a purchase on the branch. After some futile tugging and pulling, she lay back again. 'This is silly,' she told Arthur briskly. 'If you and I had a mutual understanding of each other's language I could tell you to go home and fetch someone, but that's out, isn't it? We must think of something else, and on no account must we panic.' She tugged gently at a bedraggled ear. 'Actually, I'm in a panic already and I expect you are too.' Despite herself her voice shook a little. 'Let's have another go.' She tried to wriggle on to her side, but that didn't help at all; she wriggled once more, trying to get nearer to her feet so that she could pull harder on the branches and not succeeding at all. Presently she gave up and lay back on her elbows. The storm was rolling away now, rumbling and muttering as it went, but the rain was still pelting down. No one in their senses would be out of doors in such weather—besides, the track she had taken had not the signs of much use about it. 'Oh, what's to be done, Arthur?' she asked her companion, and was surprised when he growled deep in his throat and then began to bark. He hadn't barked since he had attached himself to her, and she was suddenly frightened. Supposing it was someone who wouldn't be prepared to help her? Someone she wouldn't understand anyway. She could be robbed . . . she had no purse with her, but she was wearing a gold watch and a plain gold chain, not wildly valuable but worth something.

Arthur barked again and cocked an ear, waving his deplorable tail, and now she heard whistling—not a tune, just a whistle any man might use to call his dog, and she'd heard it before—at Hawkshead. She took a deep breath and shouted with all her might.

Charles Cresswell came out of the trees seconds later. 'All right, all right, you don't need to bawl like that,' he spoke testily. 'And why the hell are you lying there?'

The great wave of delight and relief which had warmed her ebbed away and left her cold. She said with dignity and only a very small tremor in her voice, 'Because I'm unable to get up.' The tremor threatened to get out of control. 'I have tried . . .' It would be best not to go on in case he thought she was crying. She looked away and wiped a tear away. 'I've had Arthur for company, he's been awfully good . . .'

He stood looking down at her. 'And rather more sense than I expected—I hoped he'd answer my whistle. Why are you crying?'

'I'm not!' she flared up at once. 'It's raining and I'm wet. I'd be grateful if you would pull that wretched branch off my feet. I'm very wet . . .'

He had no jacket and his shirt and slacks were sopping, his hair plastered on to his head like a grey helmet. 'So are you,' she added.

He grunted something, bending over her feet and testing the weight of the branch. 'You're not hurt?' he asked. 'You're pinned down as neatly as though you'd been measured for it. Keep very still and don't lift your feet—not so much as an inch.'

He began to pull steadily and in a few moments she was free. 'No, don't move yet!' Judith was surprised at the sharpness of his voice. He picked up each foot in turn and felt it carefully. Only when he had done that did he bend again and lift her on to them, and that surprised her still more, because she was a big girl and no light weight.

Charles made no effort to release her; he stood with his arms round her holding her close, staring down into her wet face, frowning a little.

'Why are you looking at me like that?' she demanded.

'I'm trying to remember why I didn't like you.'

'But you still don't—you told me not to bawl . . .'

'Ah, that was because I was afraid you'd been hurt—it made me angry, you see.'

'Angry?' She studied his face carefully, the cold inside her rapidly turning to a warm excited glow.

He didn't answer her but bent his head and kissed her. For a professor of Ancient History whom one would suppose to be indifferent to kissing girls, thought Judith, he was doing rather well, it was a pity that she loved him so much, even if he were beginning to like her just a little, because that wouldn't be enough.

He kissed her again, gently this time. 'I think it would be a splendid idea if we were to be married,' he observed, and smiled at her to set her heart ricocheting round her chest. 'But first we'd better get back to the villa and dry clothes.'

It was difficult to answer him. Judith debated the best way to do it and gave up. Did she say 'What a splendid idea', and would that do for both remarks, or should she answer the one about getting married? If she ignored that and said 'Yes, let's,' he might think she was referring to getting married and not to going back to the villa. She ended by saying 'Well—um . . .' and slipping out of his arms and starting to walk back along the track with Arthur trotting beside her and Charles beside her.

She reflected that she wasn't over-lucky with her proposals—the middle of the night when she was half dead on her feet, and now in a downpour of rain with the tail end of a storm still rumbling its way to the other side of the sky, and her looking like a half drowned creature, covered in mud and twigs and her hair like nothing on earth. He couldn't have meant it. And this opinion was borne out by his manner as they walked back; beyond curt warnings as to where she should walk, he remained silent. Even at the most difficult bits when he gave her an impatient hand, he had nothing to say.

By the time he had reached the villa the sky had cleared and the sun poured down once more, warming her chilled bones but not her bewildered heart. Lady Cresswell, sitting on the patio still, eyed them with interest.

'You're both very wet, my dears. Go and change quickly and tell me all about it when you have; there's just time before lunch.'

Judith went pink. 'It—it rained,' she said, quite unnecessarily, and whisked herself away without looking at Charles. She told herself fiercely that she was a fool as she showered and got into clean clothes, but that didn't stop her from putting on her make-up with extra care and brushing her hair to a shining perfection and then at the last minute changing her dress for one she hadn't worn before; handkerchief lawn in blue—it matched her eyes exactly.

The Professor and his mother were deep in talk when she went downstairs and they both turned to look at her as she joined them. He handed Judith a glass of sherry and when she had sat down, sat himself. He said quietly: 'I asked you to marry me just now, Judith, but you didn't believe me, did you? So I'll ask you again before a witness.'

Judith put down her glass with such speed that she spilt the sherry. She tingled with excitement and delight strongly tempered with resentment that this, another proposal of marriage, should be a public one. Was she never to have the romantic occasion so familiar in all the best romantic novels? She looked at Charles, who was looking at her pleasantly enough, but quite lacking that same romantic air she would have liked. The temptation to say yes at once was enormous, but she had no intention of being too eager—he had asked her to marry him, but he hadn't said he loved her . . .

She glanced at Lady Cresswell and saw that that lady's face was alive with happy anticipation. 'It's the dearest wish of my heart,' Lady Cresswell smiled at her. 'I've been hoping . . . but of course it's for you to decide, Judith.'

Judith emptied her glass and Charles filled it again without asking. 'Suppose you think about it for a bit?' he suggested. 'Maybe our trip to Monchique will help you to decide.'

And later, sitting beside him as he drove up into the mountains, she changed her mind a dozen times. Perhaps she was expecting too much, perhaps in real life men didn't say and do the things they did in books? She had always prided herself on being modern and matter-of-fact, but she suspected that she was neither. And what about Eileen Hunt? She had forgotten the wretched creature. She stared at the winding uphill road ahead.

'I have always supposed,' she said carefully, 'that you were going to marry Eileen Hunt.'

He showed no surprise at the un-expectedness of her remark. 'I can't recall ever wishing to do so,' he told her, 'I've never wanted to marry until I got to know you, Judith.'

And with that she had to be content. He began to talk about the country they were passing through, pointing out the cork trees lining the road and the great sweep of country below them with the sea in the distance. And when they reached Mon-chique village he drove slowly, allowing her to see its tiny square and the handful of shops before turning into a steep uphill road; the last stage of their drive.

Lady Cresswell, dozing on the back seat, woke up as they left the village, declaring that the scenery was as beautiful as ever and she longed for a cup of tea.

'Which we will have in a very few minutes now,' her son assured her, and presently pulled into the side of the road overlooking the forest below. The *estalagem* where they were to have tea was built into the mountainside on the opposite side of the

road, a charming little inn with a terrace
overlooking the road and the view beyond
and a friendly proprietor who ushered them
to a table and brought tea and little round
cakes. They sat for some time in the warm
sunshine while Lady Cresswell talked about
her previous visits, and presently she
insisted on taking Judith into the inn to look
around its elegant sitting room and pretty
dining room with the small bar beyond.
'I've stayed here—oh, years ago,' she
explained. 'The bedrooms are charming and
it's so peaceful, although in the summer it's
always full, of course. It would be a
splendid place for a honeymoon,' she added
hopefully.

'I'm not sure that I'm the wife for
Charles, Lady Cresswell.'

'But you are, my dear. I knew that the
moment I set eyes on you. He's difficult,
I know, and wrapped up in his work;
he doesn't suffer fools gladly and he hides
his feelings. He can be ill-tempered and
arrogant too, but I think you could deal
with that. He can't bear to be fussed over,

and you never fuss.' She smiled gently.
'You mustn't think that because he isn't
demonstrative he doesn't care.'

Which was precisely what Judith had
been thinking.

They drove on after a while, along the
gently winding road, past an occasional villa
standing in a sea of flowers, and always
orange groves on either side of them and the
mountain rose covering everything. There
were no villages, though looking down the
mountainside it was possible to see a great
sweep of country running down to the sea,
dotted with houses and an occasional town.
And finally at the top, they came out on to a
broad stretch of land, strewn with great
boulders and housing a radio station. There
was a restaurant there too and several
houses, built in a rough square, and it all
looked rather lonely. Judith, invited to get
out and have a look, did so, climbing an
outcrop of rock so that she could get a better
view. The mountains sloped away to the
plains beyond and the late afternoon sun
sparkled on the distant sea. Beautiful, but

quite unlike England, but then England
seemed so far away, as did her life there.
She knew now that she could never go back
to it, even if she didn't marry Charles, and
although she longed to do just that, she still
wasn't certain if he loved her.

He came and stood beside her on the
rocks and flung an arm around her
shoulders. 'Lonely, isn't it?' he observed,
'and beautiful too. When will you marry me,
Judith?'

His voice hadn't altered at all, he could
have been making some further remark
about the view—moreover, wasn't he
taking her for granted?

'The future will be bleak without you, my
dear.' And now his voice was warm. To her
own surprise Judith heard herself saying:
'As soon as it can be arranged, Charles, and
providing your mother keeps well.'

He dropped a light kiss on her cheek. 'I
think we'll have to make our plans as and
when we can—it does depend on the next
report, doesn't it?'

And with that she had once more to be

content. If she hadn't loved him so very much she would have resented his matter-of-fact attitude. Perhaps he would get better as time went on—after all, he had spent a good many years with his nose in books and manuscripts, none of them romantic.

But if Charles lacked romantic ideas, his mother made up for it. She was delighted when they told her presently, and the whole of the return journey was taken up with her excited plans for the wedding, although when they reached the villa she declared contritely: 'I'm being a silly interfering old woman, my dears. Of course you'll make your own plans, only I'm so happy ... I shall go to bed early, I think, and have my dinner in my room. I'm tired.'

So presently Judith went downstairs to find Charles in the sitting room waiting for her. She felt a little shy of him for a minute or two, but he greeted her with a casual friendliness, which dispelled that almost at once, enquired after his mother and went on to tell her that he intended seeing the doctor on the following morning.

'I must go back in a couple of days,' he told her, 'and it might be as well if you and Mother returned some time next week. Until then we'd better not make too many plans. Would you agree to a quiet wedding, Judith?'

She sat a little to one side of him, watching his face. He was really very good-looking, and distinguished with it—not that that mattered; she loved him with all her heart and she longed to tell him so. When they knew each other better, she would be able to do that, but not just yet; she had a feeling that he was holding her at arms length. She didn't know why, and it puzzled her a bit. He had been so anxious for her to say she would marry him, and now that she had, he seemed to have lost all interest.

'I'd rather be married quietly,' she told him.

And there the matter ended, what should have been a romantic tête-à-tête turning into a most disappointing evening, with the Professor describing mediaeval churches over dinner and going on to mediaeval bridges with sharp cutwaters. Judith, not having a clue as to what they were, looked intelligent and hoped she sounded as though she knew what he was talking about. The moment she got back to England, she would have to read up all she could about the twelfth and thirteenth centuries, because they were obviously of more importance to Charles than the present one; but she loved him so much that she was prepared to get interested in everything to do with his work. She reflected a little sadly that probably married life wouldn't be quite what she had imagined it to be. Charles would forget birthdays and anniversaries and invitations to dinner; he most likely wouldn't utter a word during breakfast and the children would have to be hushed whenever he was bogged down in a particularly sticky bit of research. But none of that mattered as long as he loved her.

She said goodnight presently, and he kissed the top of her head and hoped that she would sleep well—then suddenly swept her close and kissed her fiercely, sweeping away all her doubts.

The next morning, with Lady Cresswell settled on the patio and Charles in Silves with the doctor, Judith telephoned her mother, to be instantly engulfed in that lady's delighted exclamations. 'And when is the wedding to be?' asked her mother. 'Here, of course, darling, such a lovely church . . . what's your ring like?'

'I haven't got one yet—we're coming back to England in a week or ten days, I expect I'll get it then.' She added: 'It's all been rather sudden.'

'We'll see you soon?'

'I'll let you know, Mother—I'm not sure what's going to happen. I expect we'll discuss it today; Charles isn't going back until tomorrow.'

Lady Cresswell went to rest after lunch and Judith and Charles went into the garden and stretched out on the grass. It was hot, but in the shade of the trees the air was cooler. Judith lay back, her sunglasses perched on her pretty nose, her hat perched on the top of her head, shading her face. Arthur panted beside her, and Mrs Smith and the kittens lolled in their box. It was very quiet except for the crickets, and she felt a little sleepy, but she came awake at once when Charles rolled over and spoke.

'I've had a talk with Dr Sebastiao, he seems quite satisfied with Mother, but of course she's due for a check-up in a couple of weeks, isn't she? I've chartered a plane for Thursday week—that's ten days more or less. I'll come over the evening before that and drive us all to Faro—I'll arrange quarantine for the animals when I get back the day after tomorrow. We'd all better go straight to London and stay at Mother's flat until she's had her tests. We'll decide what to do next while we're there.'

She waited for him to say something about them getting married, but he had rolled over again and closed his eyes. She said meekly: 'Very well, Charles,' because of course he couldn't make plans yet, he would have to wait until he knew more about his mother. All the same, she stifled hurt feelings.

It was the following afternoon as she was coming downstairs after seeing Lady Cresswell settled for her nap when she heard the telephone in the sitting room ringing and crossed the hall to answer it. But Charles had come in from the patio and was already there; she heard his voice clearly saying, 'Hullo, Eileen,' and despite all her better instincts, she paused to listen—but only for a moment; eavesdroppers were on a par with other people's letter readers, and she would have no part in that. But she had taken no more than two steps when she stopped again. Charles's voice, rather pedantic and decisive, was only too easy to listen to.

'Oh, yes,' he was saying, 'I've arranged everything, although we can't make final arrangements until we're back in England. But it couldn't be more convenient. She'll be there to look after my mother, day and night, and of course mother is very fond of her. She took some persuading, but after all, she'll get a home and security for the future.' He glanced up and saw Judith standing in the open doorway and added very deliberately: 'I'll see you when I get back tomorrow.'

He put the receiver down and sauntered towards her, his hands in his pockets.

'You were talking about me,' said Judith. Her heart was hammering in her chest and she felt a bit sick.

'And . . .?' He was staring down at her, his face bland.

'Is that why you're marrying me?' she whispered from a dry throat. 'Though I think I knew that already—you see, you forgot to say that you loved me, and I wondered . . . But I thought that perhaps— well, being a historian and—very engrossed in your work, you'd got out of the habit of saying things like that.'

She thought in a detached way that he looked exactly as he had looked on the very first time they had met—furiously angry. But when he spoke there was nothing to indicate rage in his voice. Indeed he spoke very softly. 'You really believe I would use you in such a fashion?'

She wasn't thinking straight any more. 'Yes, I do—you see, it's such a sensible arrangement. Later on, when you—Lady Cresswell—doesn't need me any more, we can go our own separate ways.'

He said silkily: 'And why should I go to all this trouble?'

'Because of Lady Cresswell, of course. We both know that she's going to die soon—you want her to be happy at all costs, don't you?'

Charles looked away from her, staring into the bright sunshine through the open door. He said at length very evenly: 'I don't think there's much point in talking any more at present.' He gave her a bleak look that wrung her heart. 'Or in the future, for that matter. Marriage to someone you don't trust is about the worst mistake one can make in life, don't you agree?'

She nodded dumbly, to speak seemed an impossibility, but presently she managed it in a voice she tried to keep steady. 'You mean you don't want to marry me now?'

His face was impassive. 'Let me put it another way; we made a mistake and most fortunately discovered it in time. But there is one thing, Judith—my mother mustn't know, not yet, and it shouldn't be too difficult to let her go on dreaming. I leave tomorrow, and when I come again in ten days to fetch you both, there'll be too much to do for her to notice anything. Once we're in England and her tests are satisfactory, she might go back to her flat. Would you go with her, Judith? We shan't need to meet.'

'Yes, of course.' She raised troubled eyes to his. 'Are you very angry, Charles?'

He didn't answer her, his eyes were hard and cold and turned her to ice and she wanted to turn tail and run away, but it was he who walked away without another word.

Lady Cresswell elected to stay up for dinner that evening and Judith spent the worst two hours of her life, laughing and talking and listening to Lady Cresswell's description of her own wedding gown and discussing the probable dress she might choose for herself, and even worse was having to listen to Charles calling her his dear and speculating as to the best place for a honeymoon. There was no need, she thought fiercely, to have brought the subject up. He was a heartless monster, and far from loving him, he was the last man she wanted to see again ever. And if he thought to upset her by such conduct, then he could think again!

This buoyed her up for the remainder of the evening and gave her a heightened colour and a glitter in her eyes which made her quite breathtakingly beautiful. If she could have brought herself to do more than glance at Charles she would have seen the look in his eyes and might even have accepted his terse invitation to walk in the garden after dinner. But she didn't look, instead she went up with Lady Cresswell presently and didn't go downstairs again, and in the morning when she went down to breakfast, Charles had already left for the airport.

CHAPTER NINE

JUDITH had slept all night, something she
hadn't expected to do, but memory came
flooding back the moment she opened her
eyes; she had sat up in bed, remembering
the coldness of Charles's eyes and the awful
travesty of a convivial evening, and in a way
it was a relief to find that Charles had gone.
She wondered what Lady Cresswell would
say when she was told, but she need not
have worried. He had gone to bid his
mother goodbye in the early hours of the
morning, seeing her bedside light on from
his window. 'I expect he said goodbye to
you too, dear,' observed Lady Cresswell
happily, 'but it will only be for a few days,
so you mustn't look so downcast.'

Judith schooled her features into cheer-
fulness, assured her that the days would fly
and that yes, Charles had said goodbye to

her, although naturally enough she supplied no details but entered wholeheartedly into a lively discussion as to whether a quiet wedding meant bridesmaids or not. It wasn't difficult, she found; all she had to do was to pretend that they were discussing someone else's wedding. The difficult part was banishing Charles's loved face from her head.

She had time to sit quietly and consider what she was going to do once Lady Cresswell had gone to take her afternoon nap. She had said that she would stay until she was no longer needed, but of one thing she was certain, she didn't want to see Charles again—not once they were both back in England. She couldn't for the moment see how this was to be done. After all, Lady Cresswell supposed them to be engaged and intending to marry as soon as possible. They would have to find a good reason for putting off the wedding, and somehow her unhappy head was unable to cope with that. The whole thing really depended on Lady Cresswell's prognosis after her check-up, so there was no point in wearing herself to rags trying to think up something now. She lay back on the grass and closed her eyes and found herself thinking of Charles again. He would have to make other plans now, and be delighted to do so because he was free; he had told her that he had never wanted to marry Eileen, but he couldn't have said anything else when she had asked him, could he? She began to wonder why he had gone to the trouble of asking her to marry him when she could have looked after his mother just as well in her own home.

She frowned. Of course it would be much more convenient to have her at Hawkshead; he would be free to travel around, knowing that she was there with his mother and he would be near at hand if, and when, she took a turn for the worse; he would be able to get on with his wretched writing in peace. And see Eileen Hunt, added a small voice at the back of her head. She remembered too with enormous relief that she hadn't told Charles that she loved him, and that was

something to be thankful for. She longed to
have a good howl, but Lady Cresswell had
sharp eyes and nothing must give her the
least suspicion . . . If she lay there much
longer feeling sorry for herself she would be
in floods of tears; she got up and went along
to the swimming pool, where she took off
her sundress and dived in. Arthur jumped
in too, probably he wasn't hygienic, but he
made a pleasant companion paddling up and
down beside her. Since they had been out in
the storm together, he had become even
more attached to her. They would have to
be parted for six months' quarantine, but
after that he could stay with her for always,
and Mrs Smith and the kittens too. Lady
Cresswell would have to make room for
them in her London flat, and afterwards she
would find a job where they would be
welcome. After all there was no need to get
married, she could earn a tolerable living,
she had loving parents and Uncle Tom. She
drew an unhappy breath and began to tear
up and down the pool, leaving a bewildered
Arthur paddling round trying to catch up.

They all went to Paraia da Rocha the next day and spent it as they had done before, only this time nothing could stop Lady Cresswell from buying a vast amount of embroidered table linen for Judith. 'Because you'll want pretty things,' she declared. 'I know that Charles has a very well run household, but men do tend to leave such things to their wives—besides, he'll probably set up a second home once you're married.'

She chatted on happily, never once mentioning her own future but throwing herself enthusiastically into plans for theirs, and Judith encouraged her; she hadn't seen the little lady so happy for days.

The outing was such a success that they went to Lagos the following day. Augusto parked the car in one of the small cobbled squares and promised to remain there, and they set out on a gentle stroll round the shops. The height of the season was over now, but the town was still quite full of tourists and there were a number of shops to attract their attention.

Lady Cresswell brought porcelain, crystal glasses and still more embroidery before consenting to stop for coffee at an open-air café in the centre of the town, and then, because she was beginning to tire, Judith suggested that they should drive out on along the coast and find somewhere for lunch before going back to Silves. 'If only Charles were here,' declared Lady Cresswell, 'he would know which restaurant we should go to—they don't look anything from the outside, you know, but the food is delicious, but it's rather warm and I think it would be nicer if we could find somewhere out of town.'

Judith glanced at her with careful casualness. Her companion was indeed tired; her face was quite drawn and her colour was bad. She said with the same casual air: 'Why do we need to go any farther? We've had a lovely morning and you know Teresa always gives us a delightful lunch. We could have it on the patio and have a lazy afternoon.'

It worried her a little that Lady Cresswell agreed so readily. But after a rest and a cup of tea, the drawn look had gone and she declared that she had never felt better, although Judith wasn't entirely happy about her pallor. Indeed, she had every intention of telephoning the doctor as soon as she could do so without Lady Cresswell knowing, but to be on the safe side she suggested supper in bed and an early night, only to be frustrated by her companion's resolve to remain up until Charles should telephone. 'He said he would,' she declared, 'and he must have told you too, Judith. I couldn't possibly go to bed until he has.'

He rang half an hour later and Lady Cresswell talked happily enough for some time. Only when she said: 'Of course you're longing to talk to Judith, she's on the patio . . .' did he interrupt her to state that he would have to ring off because someone had called and would she give Judith all the usual messages. Before she could answer he had hung up.

It took Judith quite a few minutes to assure Lady Cresswell that she wasn't too upset and certainly didn't blame her for spending so much time talking to her son. He would certainly ring again, probably later that evening, she declared mendaciously, and she was quite happy to stay out of her bed until he did. Privately she admired him for the clever way he had avoided speaking to her, something which she had been dreading ever since she had rather belatedly realised that sooner or later that would be inevitable. She decided that she would have to invent a call from him so that his mother would be satisfied. She didn't like deceiving her, but after all, weren't she and Charles already doing that on a grand scale?

She slept soundly that night, rather to her surprise, and gave Lady Cresswell such a convincing account of the telephone conversation she had had with Charles that she almost believed it herself. But she couldn't have done otherwise, looking at Lady Cresswell's still pale face lighting up so happily as she listened. She had taken the precaution of ringing Dr Sebastiao before Lady Cresswell was awake, and he had promised to call that morning. 'If you could just make it a casual visit?' Judith had suggested, and been delighted that he had understood her immediately. 'I shall not alarm the lady,' he had said.

And he didn't, strolling in casually just as they were drinking their coffee in the garden, spending half an hour talking trivialities, listening to Lady Cresswell's happy chatter about the wedding. Judith walked down the drive to where he had left his car and was reassured by his opinion that her patient was as well as could be expected. 'Although a relapse can be sudden and unexpected,' he pointed out. 'Should you have any further worries you will let me know immediately and I will come. There is blood stored at the hospital and should it be necessary a transfusion can be set up at once.'

'Here?'

'If it must. It might be possible to get Lady Cresswell to hospital, but if her condition were severe, then it would have to be done here. But we are being pessimistic,

I think.' He smiled at her as they shook hands. 'I am delighted for you that you are to marry Professor Cresswell, such a distinguished man and so very clever.'

Judith thanked him quietly and wished she could have confided in him. Possibly she would never confide in anybody: it was something best buried and forgotten. She had no doubt that Charles, once his disorganised plans had been adjusted to his wishes, would forget.

They spent the rest of the day in the garden and the following morning there was a letter for Lady Cresswell from Charles. Judith, coming back from a brief walk with Arthur, found her on the patio, reading it. 'And there's one for you,' she told Judith. 'It's on the table, dear.' She glanced up as Judith hesitated. 'Why not take it into the garden to read?' she asked kindly.

And a good thing she had done just that, thought Judith a few minutes later. She had opened the envelope with a mixture of feelings; perhaps Charles wanted to marry her after all, perhaps he was going to explain his telephone conversation. It was neither of these things. The single sheet of notepaper contained only the words, 'In the normal course of events I should be writing to you.' It was signed simply with his initials. She folded it carefully and put it back in the envelope. There was no point in thinking about it, and if she did she would weep. After a minute or two she went back to the patio.

'Isn't it nice to get letters?' she observed. 'I think I like them better than phone calls.'

'You're probably right, dear, and isn't it delightful to think that in a week's time we shall be going back to England? I've loved my stay here, but now I'm anxious to get back, there's so much to look forward to.'

Judith agreed cheerfully, feeling desperate. Unlike her companion she could see nothing to look forward to.

There were other letters as well as the English papers sent up from Silves. The morning passed pleasantly enough, as did the afternoon, because it was cooler now, so that Judith was able to stroll round the garden, cutting flowers, while Lady Cresswell sat in her usual corner. They dined earlier than usual, then Lady Cresswell went to her room immediately afterwards and Judith went with her to potter round the room, hand out her pills and take her temperature. It was up a little, and so was her pulse. Judith settled her in bed with her books and papers, and promised to come in later and turn off the bedside lamp. There was nothing really wrong, but she wasn't happy about the increased temperature. She stayed up later than usual and when she paid her final visit to Lady Cresswell's room, it was to find her asleep with the book open in her hand. Judith switched off the light and went along to her own room and when she was ready for bed, opened the communicating door between them before she got between the sheets.

She was still awake when she heard the faintest of sounds from the other room. She was out of bed in a flash and switching on Lady Cresswell's light within seconds, to find her sitting up in bed, holding a handkerchief to her nose.

Judith fetched a towel, talking soothingly the while, tossing the fruit from the bowl because there was no chance to get to the kitchen and find another one, fetching more towels, propping Lady Cresswell against more pillows. She worked fast with a reassuring calm, even when she turned back the bedclothes and saw the purpura patches her voice remained even and cheerful. 'I must get some ice,' she said cheerfully. 'I'll only be two ticks, just keep the towel under your nose and stay sitting up.'

She knew the doctor's number, she had memorised it when they had first arrived. He answered at once, listened to what she had to say, told her he would be with her as soon as possible and rang off.

When she got back with the ice she could see that Lady Cresswell was on the verge of collapse. 'The doctor is coming,' she told her calmly. 'Try not to be frightened—it looks awful, I know, but it happens occasionally and stops of its own accord.'

Lady Cresswell smiled faintly. 'I have every intention of getting over this,' she said weakly. 'You see, I've made up my mind to see my first grandchild at least.'

'I'll see if we can manage twins,' Judith told her, and was glad she had, for a few minutes later Lady Cresswell lapsed into unconsciousness.

Dr Sebastiao arrived almost immediately after that and started to set up a transfusion. 'She is too ill to move, but I think we may save her.'

Judith nodded. 'Oh, we must,' she begged him, handing him what he needed, making sure that he could manage without her for a minute or two. 'I must let Charles know,' she said urgently, then flew downstairs to the telephone. It was barely eleven o'clock, he would still be up—or out. She dialled feverishly and a moment later heard his voice.

'Judith here . . .'

'Yes?' There was ice in his voice now but she didn't heed it.

'Charles—your mother has collapsed. Dr

Sebastiao is with her, giving her a transfusion—she can't be moved yet.'

The silence at the other end seemed endless. 'I'll be with you as soon as possible,' he said at length, and hung up.

She flew upstairs again, thankful that Charles hadn't wasted time with a lot of questions. There was plenty to do. She said merely to Dr Sebastiao: 'He's coming,' and rolled up the sleeves of her dressing gown.

The Professor arrived very quietly just before six o'clock in the morning, and by then Lady Cresswell was conscious and holding her own nicely. He came soft-footed into the bedroom and said, 'Hullo, Mother,' in a perfectly ordinary voice, disregarding the bottles and tubes and paraphernalia littering the place. He might have come at speed, but he didn't look as though he had; he was freshly shaved and his clothes looked as though he had just put them on—in direct contrast to Dr Sebastiao, whose chin was as blue as ink and his rather long hair quite wild. Judith looked worse, though; she had had no time to fasten her cotton gown but had wrapped it around her and tied it tight with the sash, all bunched up, and her hair was a golden tangle. There were purple shadows beneath her blue eyes and at some time during the long night she had taken her feet out of her slippers and forgotten to put them back in.

But she was unconscious of the fact. She thanked God silently that Charles had arrived and that his mother was able to greet him and then got on with what she was doing; Lady Cresswell was making a splendid recovery, but there was much to be done and a good deal of careful nursing involved. Judith hadn't stopped all night, but neither had the doctor. He was talking to Charles now, who was standing by the bed holding his mother's hand. They were speaking Portuguese, and that softly, so that she had no idea what they were saying, but presently Dr Sebastiao came over to her.

'I am going to my home now, to prepare for the day and have breakfast, but I will return in two hours. I think Lady Cresswell is safely through her relapse, but the transfusion must continue for the rest of the day and I will do a blood count when I come back. I have the two we have already taken and they will be checked at the hospital. I no longer fear for her life, but she will need constant care. Shall I send a nurse to help you?'

'If I can get a couple of hours' sleep now I shall be quite all right for the rest of the day, but perhaps you'd better ask Professor Cresswell.'

Certainly there must be a second nurse she heard Charles say, perhaps the doctor would be so good as to bring her with him when he came again?

He didn't look at Judith when he spoke, indeed, he hadn't done more than glance at her since he had arrived, but she had been too busy to think about that. She listened quietly to Dr Sebastiao's instructions and finished what she was doing before departing to the kitchen, where Teresa was making tea, to fetch a refreshing drink for her patient.

When she got back, the doctor had gone

and Charles took the tray from her. 'Eat something,' he ordered in a no-nonsense voice, 'go to bed for an hour and then come back here. Tell me what I have to do, and if I'm worried I'll fetch you.'

She shook off her tiredness. 'I'm perfectly all right, thank you—a cup of tea . . .'

He interrupted her ruthlessly. 'You hardly inspire confidence looking as you do now. Do as I say!'

Judith brushed past him, took Lady Cresswell's pulse, saw that she had fallen into a light sleep, and went away without a word. If she had started to speak, she wouldn't have stopped, she would probably have shouted at him, thrown a vase at his arrogant head . . . How dared he? She looked down at her rumpled person; what had he expected? Starched uniform and smooth hair under a cap and never mind the patient's condition worsening with every minute? She flew downstairs. 'I hate him!' she told herself. 'He's a monster, I hope he marries Eileen and lives miserably ever after!'

She drank hot tea in the kitchen, answering the anxious Teresa as best she could while she gobbled rolls and butter. And back in her room she set her alarm clock for an hour's sleep, had a shower and tumbled into bed. It seemed that no sooner had she closed her eyes than she was opening them again, but once she was up and dressed she felt better for her short rest. She dressed in a sleeveless cotton dress, thrust her feet into sandals, tied back her hair and went into Lady Cresswell's room.

Lady Cresswell was still asleep and the Professor was sitting by the bed watching her. He looked tired now and remote. He got up when he saw Judith, said: 'I'll go and have something to eat, she hasn't stirred,' and had gone before she could say a word.

Judith thought it was a good thing in a way, for if she had given him sympathy, he might have thought she was holding out the olive branch. That was the last thing she wanted, she told herself firmly, and the last thing he wanted too.

Lady Cresswell stirred and woke before

long, so that she was able to bathe her face and hands and tidy her hair. Lady Cresswell frowned at the drip above her head. 'How long do I have to have that revolting thing?' she demanded in a weak voice, 'and where's Charles?' and before Judith had a chance to answer her: 'You've been up all night, my dear, you must be worn out.'

'It'll come down later today if Dr Sebastiao is satisfied with you. Charles is downstairs having breakfast, and I'm not in the least tired. Don't talk too much, Lady Cresswell, you're doing fine, but you've some lost ground to make up.'

'Bless you, child!' Her eyes went to the door and she smiled. 'Charles—you got here so quickly. Have you had any sleep?'

He assured her that he had, although Judith very much doubted that. 'And don't tire yourself with talking, Mother,' he begged her.

'I feel better,' she smiled faintly at him. 'And I'm going to get better—I told Judith, I want to see my first grandchild—she's promised to make it twins.' She closed her eyes and dozed and Judith, her head bent over the pad she was using for keeping her records, went scarlet. After a moment she lifted her head defiantly and looked him in the eye.

'Well, it made her happy,' she said softly.

He didn't answer her; she hadn't expected him to, and since Dr Sebastiao arrived just then, the awkward moment passed.

He had brought a nurse with him, a tall dark, serious girl with just enough English to get by. Judith lost no time in convincing the doctor that it would be better for her to do night duty; during the day the Professor would be there to smooth any small difficulties, and at night, if Lady Cresswell couldn't sleep she would be able to read to her. 'Six o'clock until six o'clock?' she asked briskly and since the nurse agreed, the matter was settled at once, much to her relief; she would only have to meet Charles for the briefest of periods morning and evening, for in the morning she could eat her breakfast and have a quick swim when she got off duty, and be in bed long before he was up.

She listened to all that the doctor had to say, made sure that the nurse knew where everything she might need could be found, arranged with Teresa that the simple diet the doctor had ordered should be ready at the times he had suggested, and lastly telephoned to London to Lady Cresswell's own doctor. It was the Professor who took the phone from her. As she turned away, he said: 'I'm greatly in your debt, Judith.'

She mumbled something and hurried upstairs. Five minutes later she was in the swimming pool and very shortly after that sitting at the kitchen table eating her breakfast while Teresa clucked in a motherly way round her.

She was very tired and slept right through the day until Teresa came in with a cup of tea and pointed to the clock. Judith sat up and yawned, then jumped out of bed, and less than an hour later she went along to Lady Cresswell's room, bathed, neatly dressed, her hair just so, and a good meal inside her, feeling ready to tackle any emergency that might arise during the night.

Lady Cresswell had had a good day, Lucia, the nurse, told her. Dr Sebastiao had been and would come again in an hour's time. The patient was dozing again, taking the nourishment she was offered and was quite reconciled to the transfusion remaining up until the present bottle was finished. From the manner in which this was said, Judith guessed that Lady Cresswell had been a bit difficult about that. She wished Lucia a good night, urged her to go straight to the kitchen where Teresa was waiting with her supper tray, and set herself to putting the room in order for the night.

It was still a lovely day, with the early evening sun nicely tempered with a cool breeze. Judith drew back the shutters gently so that Lady Cresswell would see the garden when she woke up and lingered a minute at the windows. Of Charles there was no sign, but she hadn't expected to see him; he would keep out of her way as much as possible, she was sure of that.

Dr Sebastiao came an hour later, looked over the record Judith had written of pulse, temperature, and blood pressure, and pronounced himself satisfied. Certainly the blood pressure was rising nicely and there was almost no fever. He beamed at Judith, and patted her on the shoulder.

'We have been lucky this time, Judith.' She glanced at the sleeping figure in bed. He went on, 'I have been in consultation with her own doctor in London and he thinks that as soon as she is able, she should return to hospital in London for a thorough check-up, with care, she could live a year, perhaps two, who can say?' He put his stethoscope back in his bag. 'I shall not wake her—will you check carefully and let me know if there is anything not as it should be. I will go and speak with the Professor.'

He wished her a quiet goodnight and went downstairs. So Charles was in the house, keeping out of her way. Her heartache was so real that she could only stand still and let it wash over her.

'Judith!' Lady Cresswell's thin voice switched a smile on to her face as she turned towards the bed.

'Hullo,' she said cheerfully. 'Dr Sebastiao's just gone; he's very pleased with you.'

'You looked so sad—is something the matter.'

'Heavens, no—everything's just fine. I'm to take the drip down as soon as it's finished, you'll be glad of that, won't you? It may wake you up while I'm doing it, but I'll be as quiet about it as I can.'

'Yes, dear. Where's Charles—you've had no time to be together.'

Lady Cresswell sounded fretful and Judith said at once: 'Oh, yes, we manage—besides, we've got all the time in the world, haven't we? He's downstairs with the doctor. Now I'm going to give you a drink and do one or two chores, and you're going back to sleep.'

'I'm glad you're here at night, Judith. It's

not so bad during the day, but at night I get afraid . . .'

Judith perched carefully on the side of the bed and took a frail hand in hers. 'Well, don't—there's no need, it all boils down to the simple fact that you've had a severe nosebleed and the quickest way to get over it was to keep you quiet in bed and give you a spot more blood. You're going to be as right as rain in no time at all; you'll have your check-up when we get back to England and you'll be none the worse.'

It was almost midnight and Lady Cresswell had been sleeping peacefully for some time when the Professor came quietly into the room. He looked bone weary, and Judith had to suppress a strong desire to go to him and throw her arms round his neck and comfort him; instead she said nothing at all.

He looked at his mother and then at her, his eyebrows raised in query.

'Yes, she's sleeping soundly. I'm going to take the drip down in a very short time.' Judith kept her voice pleasantly professional.

'In that case, will you come on to the balcony for a moment?'

It was dark there and she was thankful that he couldn't see her face; he most likely had something nasty to say to her.

'I have to thank you for all you're doing for Mother,' he told her, his voice nicely schooled to politeness. 'It's awkward that I should have to return so soon, I must ask you to continue the pretence of our engagement for the time being.'

His face was in the shadow, but the cool indifference of his voice turned her cold. 'Yes, of course.'

She could think of nothing else to say, and as he remained silent she went back into the bedroom and checked the drip, thankful that she would be kept busy for a few minutes, taking it down. It was annoying that he didn't go away, but sat down in a chair a little way from the bed and picked up a book. Really, the man had no feelings at all! she thought crossly as she started to dismantle the drip. Lady Cresswell woke for a moment as she took out the cannula and whispered: 'Where's Charles?'

'Sitting in the chair in the corner,' said Judith promptly, and she went to sleep again, satisfied.

Judith tidied away the mess, checked her patient and went to sit down on the high-backed chair near the bed. She had letters to write and she might as well go on with them, but she had scarcely started when the Professor said from his corner: 'You'll find your supper on a tray in the kitchen—go and eat it, I'll stay here until you return.'

She started to say: 'But I can eat my supper here...' when he interrupted her.

'Do as you're told, Judith.' Just for a second there was a gleam of amusement in his eyes. 'We don't want to disturb Mother, do we?'

She got up without a word and he opened the door for her. As she passed him their hands brushed against each other; it was like an electric shock to her and she fled down the stairs as though running for her life.

In the kitchen she pulled herself together

and sat down at the table to eat the meal
Teresa had prepared. She was all kinds of a
fool and thank heaven she wouldn't have to
see much of him. He would surely go to bed
soon and she would be in her own bed long
before anyone else was up in the morning.
She made tea and drank the pot dry, and
thus fortified went back upstairs.

The Professor was sitting in his chair,
reading. He got up as soon as Judith went in
and said goodnight, then went away; which
left her the rest of the night to think about
him and wonder if she had been too hasty.
Perhaps he hadn't meant quite all he said
when Eileen had telephoned, perhaps she
should have given him the chance to
explain, but if she had been mistaken, why
had he been so quick to break off everything
between them? Her head ached with the
muddle of her thoughts and she was glad
when Lady Cresswell woke up soon after
five o'clock and she could get busy with
early morning chores. They were enjoying a
cup of tea together when Lucia joined them.
Judith waited only long enough to give her

report and wish Lady Cresswell a good day, before leaving them together. She was beset by the fear that Charles would turn up before she could escape.

She was tired, and hot and hungry and she decided to shower, get into her nightie and dressing gown, have a quick breakfast and go straight to bed, but down in the kitchen the faithful Arthur got out of his basket, inviting her to go outside, so she drank some orange juice from the fridge, picked up a roll from the table and opened the back door.

The morning was enchanting, the light still pearly and the early sun shedding a gentle warmth. Judith sat down on the grass, well away from the house, and kicked off her slippers. Arthur flopped down beside her and in a few minutes they were joined by Mrs Smith and the kittens, anxious for company and on the look-out for breakfast. Judith shared her roll and sat chewing at the bit which remained, but presently she gave up and sat, the bread still in her hand and her knees under her chin, staring ahead of her, not seeing the garden round her, only a bleak future of years without Charles. Until that moment she had managed not to cry, but now her feelings got the better of her and tears poured down her cheeks in an absolute torrent.

She sniffed and sobbed for a few minutes, then caught her breath at Arthur's welcoming whine and the busy swish of his tail. He didn't do that for Augusto or Teresa; he was still a little wary of them and he ignored the doctor when he came to the house; he whined like that for herself, Lady Cresswell and Charles. So it had to be Charles. Judith turned round slowly, quite forgetful of her wet blotchy face, and saw him standing there within a few paces of her. He didn't look as though he had slept a wink, although he was shaved and immaculate. Indeed, he looked every day of his years but nonetheless strikingly handsome in a haggard kind of way.

She could suddenly bear it no longer. She cried: 'Oh, Charles you mustn't worry so much, Lady Cresswell is going to be all right and once she's over this she'll probably be well for months, even years.'

He came towards her. 'I know that, and I'm not worried.' He sounded harsh and angry and she leaned away from him, clutching her roll. He bent down and took it from her and handed it to Arthur, then hauled her to her feet. 'I've been awake all night,' he told her testily, 'making up speeches, and now I'm here I find that none of them is suitable. There are no words . . .' he caught her close, crushing her ribs most painfully, and began to kiss her. It was, she decided, quite useless to stop him, and anyway, she didn't want to.

'I'm too old for you,' he stated severely, 'I have an infernal temper and I like my way . . .'

'None of these matter,' said Judith, 'because I love you more than enough to put up with all of them, only you haven't yet said you love me, you know.' She gave him a severe look. 'Nor did you choose to explain . . .'

'Oh, my darling, of course I love you—I fell in love with you the moment I set eyes on you in my kitchen, but nothing went right, did it? You shied away from me like a startled fawn.'

Judith chuckled. 'I'm a bit big for a fawn,' she pointed out.

'You're exactly right, every inch of you.' He kissed her again. 'And it wasn't you I was talking about but an indigent second cousin who's only too eager to live with Mother and look after her.'

'Oh!' Judith glowed with happiness, 'but she should be near us, so that we can see her as often as possible.'

'Well, she will be. There's a charming house in Hawkshead—your Uncle Tom is dealing with the buying of it for me, so you can see her every day if you want to.' He added wickedly: 'The twins will love visiting Granny.'

'The twins . . . Oh, that was to make her happy.'

'Well, it will make me happy too, my love.'

She had the horrid feeling that she was going to cry again, only this time it was because she was so happy. 'I've been very silly,' she said in a small voice.

'Indeed you have.' Though it didn't sound as though he minded that. 'But it was my fault—you see, I wasn't sure that you loved me enough.'

'More than enough, dearest Charles,' Judith assured him, and lifted her face for his kiss. Presently she asked: 'But why did Eileen telephone here?'

'Good God, darling, must we keep on talking about the girl? Remember my cousin—you met him at my house—he and Eileen see a lot of each other. It was he who remembered the indigent cousin's address and gave it to me, and he asked Eileen to phone me to see if everything had been settled.'

'You could have explained . . .'

'My dearest Miss Golightly, could we not forget the whole unfortunate matter?'

'All right, I'll never say another word,

only if you annoy me I daresay I'll mention it just once in a while, you know!'

'As long as it's not too often,' observed Charles, and fell to kissing her once more.

THE END

THESE ARE THE OTHER TITLES
TO LOOK OUT FOR
THIS MONTH

NURSE RHONA'S ROMANCE
by Anne Vinton

Rhona was disappointed, though not heart-broken, when her romance with Chris Willson came to nothing; all the same, she was glad to have her work as a district nurse to take her mind off things. And she was even more thankful for her career when her next romance, with Dr Alex Denham, crashed to disaster.

THE TRODDEN PATHS
by Jacqueline Gilbert

In the three years that had passed since she had last seen Nat Beaumont, Imogen had had plenty of time to think about their relation-ship. Had it been her fault that they had broken up – or was her father at the bottom of it? And how would she cope now that she was being forced into Nat's company again?

EACH MONTH MILLS & BOON PUBLISH
THREE LARGE PRINT ROMANCES
FOR YOU TO LOOK OUT FOR,
AND ENJOY. THESE ARE THE TITLES
FOR NEXT MONTH

———————— ✳ ————————

DISHONEST WOMAN
Jessica Steele

WIPE AWAY THE TEARS
Patricia Lake

VALLEY OF LAGOONS
Kerry Allyne